Waves

By T.P.Scott

ISBN 978-1-9163556-3-7

www.tpscottauthor.co.uk

www.twitter.com/tpscottauthor

www.facebook.com/tpscottauthor

Contents

Prologue

It was just after 8:00 p.m. on a Friday evening as I was walking along a dimly lit street trying to find the nearest tube station. I thought to myself, "Surely, this must be the way" as I turned yet another corner. I could have sworn I had just walked around this same corner only a few minutes earlier. I was in London, a city I didn't really know and only had a general idea of where the tube station was located. Looking at my watch to check the time, I noticed the battery had died. That's when I let out a deep sigh uttering "Fuck" but a little too loudly, I'd say, as a man smoking outside of a pub looked at me. His eyes narrowed as he glanced in my direction. Obviously, I tried to avoid eye contact. He looked to be maybe mid-fifties sporting a long overcoat and holding a pint of what looked to be a bitter ale in one hand. This was outside a classic east end pub that had a few dirty window and a couple of regulars chattering about within its walls. I imagined it's not one of those places that unknowns like me should ever enter. The "Red Lion" was stencilled in red letters on the sign that flapped about in the wind just below the eave to the entrance. I quickly made a mental note to never come back here. Looking at the ground, I immediately picked up my pace and carried on. In the distance, I could see bright lights and hoped this was my destination that contained some friendlier, less threatening people. As I reached into my pocket to pull out my phone to look at the time, it showed 20:21. My train was due to arrive in just 30 minutes. Opening up Google maps, it instantly located me and confirmed that I was indeed heading in the right direction towards the tube station. I must admit, I was relieved to get out of these dark back streets. I was in a great mood with a bounce in my step and felt like I was walking on air. Why? Well, the reason that I was even in the great Capital City of London is that I just had an interview with GREYSOFT! Yes, that's right. I had interviewed to become one of their lead programmers of their next game creation. I can't disclose any more than that for legal reasons but I was very excited! This was my dream come true! I had wanted to be a programmer since I was a child and finally, I was on my way to achieving that dream. I could not believe how great my interview went and how well the interviewer and myself got on. I had managed to control my anxiety apart from the fact my shirt could have been rung out like a wet dish rag afterwards. I was feeling on top of the world and nearly wanted to break into a musical number. Thinking back on that moment, I was unable to hide the smile crawling across my face and walked on in the direction of the lights.

I followed Google maps for about 100 yards but as I walked this final stretch, something felt weird and not quite right. A strange feeling immediately overcame my desire to break out in a happy dance and I suddenly felt uneasy. I could not describe it nor its source but it stopped me in my tracks. As I stopped, I noticed a girl about 5'7" with blonde hair and I'm guessing just a little older than me. She was wearing a blue denim skirt, black tights and a pullover hoodie. She was just standing there motionless staring up at the sky. I began to shrug it off as this being London, you do see the occasional oddity. Normally I would carry on but I was kind of intrigued at to what she was looking at.

"Hey, excuse me, are you ok?" I asked her. She didn't move and didn't even acknowledge me. I instantly thought it was rather rude of her but she didn't give off that sort of air so I repeated myself a little more assertively this time. "Hey, excuse me, is everything ok?" She didn't say a word but raised her arm towards the sky and extended her finger pointing just over a brightly lit building in the distance. I craned my neck skywards but couldn't really see anything interesting and especially from the lights of the building somewhat blinding me but then my eyes adjusted. I wasn't sure exactly what I was looking at but something came into focus. The best way that I can describe it would be to say that it looked like a small ball of fire with an odd blue glow with a trail of fire behind it. I had never seen anything like it. "What the hell is that" I asked with an almost instantly dry throat. At this point, she turned to me looking mesmerised and quietly said "I have no idea. I was just looking up at the stars and noticed it. Do you think it's a plane on fire or perhaps a shooting star?" I didn't know so I just kept staring up at the sky trying to sort it out but admitted that I had absolutely no idea. At this point, I did what any normal person would do living in the 21st century and grabbed my phone to take a picture. I even thought about doing some sort of Facebook live video update. I snapped what I thought was a fairly good picture and then started recording to upload to my YouTube channel. Little did I know in that moment that not too long after, this video would stand at

255,567,987 views on a night that was about to change the world forever.

We both continued to stand there watching as this ball of fire move across the sky in what seemed to be slow motion. Why has it not fallen from the sky by now? It seemed to be getting lower and lower and could clearly now see that it was certainly not a plane. The blue glow surrounding this ball of fire grew brighter as it neared the ground. I was now really starting to panic and looked to the pretty girl beside me thinking "God damn, I wish I had some antiperspirant right about now" as I could feel my anxiety rising and was starting to sweat. "Did I smell?", I thought to myself. Other questions rattling around in my head were what could I say to this girl, what the hell was this thing, shouldn't it have burned up by now, was I in danger? These thoughts kept going around and round and I was quickly getting lost in my own thoughts. I was panicked, nervous, scared, several hundred miles from home and worst of all, I was probably starting to smell badly beside a beautiful girl. Suddenly, I was brought back to reality with a loud BANG as a car a little further down the road, crashed into the back end of a taxi. I quickly spun about 360 degrees and did a quick view of everything all around me. I had been so lost in my own head that I now saw that everyone was looking skywards. They were all standing as still as could be and obviously had dropped what they were doing to try and sort what was going on in the sky as well. Even the man that I saw earlier in the pub doorway that had been staggering down the street behind me, dropped his cigarette in disbelief. In an instant, I forced myself back to the present and turned to this girl whose name I didn't even know and grabbed her arm saying, “I think we better move away from here”. She shrugged me off and looked a little taken back. I guess I can’t blame her since a strange man was grabbing at her. All of a sudden, the entire sky above us lit up with a blinding light and then it happened. The moment that would change the world as we know it.

We had no idea what we had just witnessed as it was instantly and eerily quiet. But then just as quickly, that tiny moment of silence was gone as in the distance, a massive cloud of fire rose from the ground. It looked like a volcano erupting and must have extended 100 feet or more into the night sky as if it was daylight. “OH MY GOD”, I shouted aloud unable to hide my anxiety any longer. I’d forgotten that my phone was still recording all of this. It seemed that whatever had hit the ground was about 2 to 3 miles away but fire, smoke and debris was rolling towards us rapidly in what seemed like waves. I couldn’t move. It was like I was frozen in shock and disbelief like I was watching some Sci-fi film. But what I thought was just a nightmare quickly became reality when it reached me in a matter of seconds from impact. I was knocked off my feet and sent flying backwards onto the ground. Everything seemed to be happening in slow motion just as my head hit the sidewalk with a sickening crunch and everything went dark.
When I finally opened my eyes after what seemed like an eternity to me, I tried to sit up but my God, my head was throbbing. Fighting through the pain, I managed to prop myself up enough to survey the area around me. I had landed about 5 feet from where I had been standing. I looked down at my body to make sure it was all still

intact and noticed a massive rip in my nice, new suit. I just bought it yesterday, dammit. I had dressed nicely for my interview wearing a white shirt, a skinny black tie and smart black shoes. I wanted to look my best for my interview even though I would've rather been wearing a geek top, jeans and Converse. My phone had been thrown a few feet away so I crawled towards to see if it was still functioning as I'd obviously need to call for help. As I grabbed at this odd little device that was still recording, I remembered the girl. Where was she? Was she ok? I peered through the smoke hovering over everything and as my eyes adjusted a bit, I saw her. She seemed dazed and confused as I but was moving about and groaning. "Well, at least she's alive", I thought. I looked down the street in front of me as far I could manage and couldn't believe what I was seeing. The car that I had just seen reared a taxi was now on its roof. People were screaming. Car alarms screaming from every direction. Chaos was everywhere as far I could see. Buildings with their windows blown out and shattered glass covering the ground and I'm assuming some people, too. The air was filled with dust making it difficult to see and to breathe. My senses and my anxiety were on overload to say the least. I then looked behind me and noticed a man that had been blown backwards into a railing which had impaled him directly through his chest. I hoped that perhaps he was only badly injured but as I struggled to my feet to help him, I checked his pulse and there wasn't one. I let out a small gasp as I'd never seen or touched a dead person before and will admit at this point, I was a little sick in my mouth. I choked it back instantly regretting that decision as the taste was bitter. What the hell has happened? Was it terrorism? Had a missile landed? Had the

Russians finally attacked? Was it a plane crash? But surely a plane crash wouldn't have that sort of impact. It had to be a missile. I was convinced of it. Trying to be somewhat brave, I turned to the girl and asked "Are you ok?" as calmly as I could manage. She looked at me with an awkward but cute smile and said, "Well, I'm alive so that's a plus, I guess. How about you?"

"Yeah, I think so", I replied as I checked the back of my head for any blood. My adrenaline was fading and the pain was starting to surface. Then the girl near me let out a scream. She had looked back and seen the man impaled on the post. I moved towards her putting my hand on hers and did my best to reassure her everything was going to be ok. But who was I kidding? I didn't think it would be at all and I was scared, in pain and there was a dead man right behind me. I realised my words to her seemed empty but I hoped that in some way, they reassured her. As I looked down at her trembling hands, I noticed a small cut so I pulled a napkin from my pocket and tried my best to clean it up for her. We just sat there for a moment just trying to take it all in; however, for some strange reason my mind wandered to video games and how this would be an awesome beginning for one. My mind had a strange habit of going off on its own at the strangest of times. If this was a game, I thought, then surely at this stage I would have a big gun in one hand, muscles on top of my muscles and be some sort of super cool marine. Then my brain switched gears a bit. I thought, "What would one of my film heroes like Arnie do?" Well, he would dust himself off, say some smart one liner and probably swing the girl over his shoulder and be the hero of the hour. Unfortunately, this was neither film nor game. This was real life that I was snapped back to by the loud sirens of police cars and ambulances coming from behind me rushing past and out of view. Unknown to me at that time, an estimated 12,000 people were now dead. We still didn't know what happened. Just that something terrible did. As I helped this girl to her feet, we decided to set off to see what we could find out. Later on, we would find out that this area, this ground that we now stood upon that was in shambles and chaos would become known as "Impact Zero" and would be described as "Wave One" bringing with it, one of the greatest challenges to date that humanity has faced with survival. But I'm getting ahead of myself......

Chapter I - Impact

"FUCK" is all that was playing round in my head as I tried to get my bearings. I mean, what do I do? I had to keep reminding myself that this wasn't a film or a game. This was real. This was actually happening and I had to do something now. My thoughts were broken as she grabbed at my arm and pointed up in the sky. Oh, no. Please tell me this isn't about to happen again. I looked up and all I could utter was "Shit! There's another one! We need to move NOW! This one looks like it's headed right for us!" I grabbed her hand and we ran back the way I had come, past the pub and up some side streets. I had no idea where we were. I was just trying to outrun more destruction to some place safer. I looked back over my shoulder to see that it was heading right for us. I started to think about the inevitable. This was it. This is how I die. Of course, it just had be on the best day of my life. I was going to start living my dream with a new job and I had a lovely girl holding my hand and now I was going to die. Bloody typical as if something couldn't go right for a change. But I let my anxiety take over as I felt this was an extreme situation. I tried to think better thoughts like maybe we'll avoid it. But then, how the hell would we survive this by simply running? Surely whatever this object is, is moving faster than we are. I would never let her know this but all of this running was starting to get to me and I was struggling a bit as she was obviously a lot fitter than me. I started to curse all of the nights that I sat inside gaming, eating takeaway with my friends and washing it all down with cider. I was so glad when she started to slow down as we passed a building that looked like a large gymnasium but with windows and a swimming pool. I looked inside and couldn't see anyone there.

Just a little further up the street, I could see people huddled around a window standing very still looking at the front of an appliance store. Ah, I bet something is on the news so up we ran to join them. My suspicions were confirmed. They were all staring at a television which was showing BBC news with the subtitles scrolling. As I read them, the blood drained from my body and I felt numb. "Thousands of dead. Unknown major incident in London. No further details known at present. Stay tuned for more" followed by "Residents are advised to stay inside and off of the roads allowing emergency services to attend the scene." They were showing very grainy camera footage of whatever this object was hitting central London. In fact, it directly hit the houses of Parliament, almost like that was its intended target. This grainy footage was followed by a massive flash of light, just like the one that we saw, then the camera stopped. This same bit of news was repeated over and over again. We stood and watched for a moment just to be certain we had not missed anything else and almost forgetting that above our heads was a rather large object coming straight for us. I knew we had to find some place to hide. But whatever this object was would no doubt level the general area so what could possibly keep us safe? I glanced back at the gymnasium. Just then, for some reason, a scene from the action film "The Rock" (one of my favourite films ever) popped into my head. You know, the one where Stanley Goodspeed jumps into the river to avoid a napalm blast. Could this really work when it's not done by Hollywood? What better options do I have at this point anyway? We're already dead. What do I have to lose? Unbeknownst to me, I muttered out loud "Nothing." The girl turned to me and asked, "What did you say?" in a quiet yet confused tone. I quickly explained my idea to her and we ran back towards the gymnasium. As we bolted through the front door, she stopped. "Hey, before I die, I guess you should at least know my name so you know what to put on my headstone. I'm Summer. What's your name?" I did think this was a strange time to exchange pleasantries but since we were about to die, what the hell. "My name is Matthew. Nice to officially meet you Summer. Shall we continue on now?" I ushered her towards the pool entrance. There was absolutely nobody about as everyone had left. I looked all around as we stood in the entrance way to the swimming pool area. There was a ticket booth to the left with one of those annoying gates that had the 3 prongs that you always get stuck in when you try to walk through. To the right was a vending machine selling inflatable arm floaties and goggles. I took a deep breath and just hurdled the gate rather than try to walk through. This played out cooler in my head as I caught my foot on one of the prongs and toppled over as I landed. "Could this day get any worse?", I whispered to myself. I turned around to see Summer trying not to laugh but also a little unsure about trying this herself now. She decided to crawl underneath it. As we approached the pool and stopped at the edge, Summer turned to me with a cheeky grin and said, "Well, Matthew, we need get these clothes off before we jump in. Otherwise, we will find it hard to swim". Here I was about to get semi-naked with a beautiful girl that I just met about 2 hours ago. I was about to start my dream job. And now I am going to die. I concluded that this was the best worst day of my life.

What the hell. We both stripped down to our underwear and I couldn't help but stare at her for a moment. She was more beautiful than I imagined. Her body was gorgeous. She was fit but strong with feminine curves that I could imagine grabbing onto and her blonde hair glistened in the ever-increasing light. "This is weird", I thought. Here I am about to die but also pretty turned on. What a strange mix of emotions! Luckily, I had worn some new, tight boxer shorts so I knew that at least I looked somewhat decent even if I didn't have the best body. The pool was rather large, maybe just shorter than an Olympic sized pool. There were lanes set out for the more serious swimmers, I assumed. I spotted some floatation devices, rubber rings and the such and was relieved as I couldn't swim. I was honestly terrified of the thought of jumping in the pool and drowning. But choice did I have? Burn up in a blaze of fire or drown? Neither sounded fun or fair options. I guess I'll take my chances with the water. After all, I'm guessing Summer can swim and maybe she can help me back up for air. I looked around at the tiled walls in the room we were standing in. The changing rooms were to the left-hand side just past that annoying 3 prong gate thing that made me look like a fool. There with a few deck chairs alongside the left edge of the pool and a small slide beside the shallow end. Why weren't we near the shallow end? Could I run there right now or would I look like a chicken in front of Summer? There were 2 lifeguard platforms at either end of the pool but no lifeguards in sight. I sure could use one in a few minutes. As I looked around, what struck me was the eerie silence. All that could be heard was the hum of the fluorescent lights that dotted around the room. We were standing at the deep end of the pool both seemingly holding our breath as we waited for the final moments before impact before diving into the water. I mean, all I had to do was hold my breath, submerge and all would be good, right? That's what I keep telling myself, anyway. For the first time in this building, I looked directly up and the roof was made of what looked like glass. The sky was red getting red. It almost looked like it was on fire. It was mesmerizing if one can be mesmerized by imminent death. Then the fireball zoomed overhead and appeared to be so low that I could reach out and touch it. Then it happened. A deafening blow followed by a blinding white light. This was it. I grabbed Summer's hand, gave her one last look and we jumped. I'm not sure what depth we were at, maybe 3 meters, but I looked up to see the roof collapsing. It seemed to be falling in slow motion. I could have sworn that I could see the individual shards of glass twinkling as they shattered. Was this the end of me? Had this crazy plan worked? Had Hollywood been lying to me all of these years? I was about to find out.

Chapter II - Gamer

While I'm trying to not die right now, I should probably explain a bit more about who I am in case someone may actually care if I don't make it out of this situation. My name is Matthew. Matthew Black, actually. I am 21 years old, single and I live in the wonderful city of Newcastle. Yes, we say "Wey aye, man" or "Byker Grove" at this point. I live there with my 3 closest friends: Ross, Jon and Paul. I am 5'9" with short dark hair, average build and a little bit of a beard. I've always wanted to work in the gaming industry so I figured a beard would be a good place to start. I mean, I am also a little bit lazy but that's not the point. My friends and I are all university graduates and we met while studying for our Computer Degrees. We instantly became good friends over the duration of the course and we cemented our lasting friendship one night when we decided to have a bit of a FIFA/pizza night at my mum's place. We set it up like a tournament: winner stays on, there were tables and even a finale. It's still talked about to this day. Every time we get drunk, have a night in or have friends over, we talk about this epic night of FIFA. It's almost like folklore. Sometimes I like to think that they might write a fable of it one day. Now, if you were to talk to any of us on an individual basis, we will all say that we are the best at FIFA (as you would expect). But I'll be the first to come clean and say that I know it's not me. I'm what I've always described as a bit of a 'jack of all trades, master of none' when it comes to gaming. I have my PS4, my XBOX and my PC to game on so I can usually be found on one of those. I never hone my skills on just one game. One minute, I'm playing a racing game then it could be a sports game, a 4x grand strategy game, a first-person shooter game. Basically, I will play just about anything apart from puzzles or horror games as I am even more rubbish at both. I briefly mentioned my YouTube channel earlier. Wait a second, where was my phone? I'm hoping it's still in my suit pant pocket. But yes, I have a semi successful gaming channel on YouTube where I upload videos. Before my interview with GREYSOFT, I did some freelance programming and also worked in a local coffee shop. I enjoyed the coffee shop for the most part but every day, I sat there serving yet another stony-faced customer a latte or an espresso with some stale cake. The worst part was having to listen to yet another story about how late the trains are running or their boring day at the office. I was about to go insane! So that's when I decided to apply to GREYSOFT and make something of my life. Did I really want to move to the big smoke ("London", as some people may know it)? Did I pass this interview and would I be given the job? Did I have enough skills to make it to stage 3 of the interviews? I decided that I didn't have much keeping me up in Newcastle so a new adventure in London would be pretty cool. I did worry that maybe then I would become one of these business type lads in a cheap suit that annoys baristas on a daily basis about the train priced going up. God no, please. I shuddered at this thought!

I was born and raised in Newcastle and lived there all my life. My parents divorced when I was young and I was the eldest of my 2 other siblings so I basically helped to raise them. My younger brother still lives at home. When I left home, I went to the university as soon as I could. I attended Newcastle University and moved into the student digs mainly because it was close by and had a good reputation but also so I could be out on my own. I was happy that I was accepted at the university and on the whole, I loved my 3 years there. I'll never forget my first day, though. I was so very nervous. See, I suffer from social anxiety and had been diagnosed with depression so the thought of starting the university was the most stressful decision that I had made to that point. I remember standing at the door of the classroom terrified to turn the handle. I was unsure what lay behind the door. I started to panic and backed off a bit and just stared at the door. Suddenly, the door became a hurdle and a seemingly immovable obstacle. I put my head in my hands and just stood there. But I could NOT let anxiety beat me this time. "You can do this", I said out loud and immediately thought of the Shia LeBeouf video shouting "Just do it". I remembered his words: "Don't let your dreams be dreams. Yesterday, you said tomorrow... just do it". I took a deep breath and walked towards the door and turned the handle. In front of me, there stood a man who introduced himself as "Mr. Gormley". He was a tall, elderly gentleman with grey hair and sporting a cardigan that made him look like he belonged in the 1980's. He then said, "I'm guessing you are here for the class introduction for the computing course so please have a seat". I was a bit embarrassed that I was late coming in so I looked down at the floor as I walked to an empty area of the room to sit and as I did, I noticed that I was wearing my converse, skinny jeans a t-shirt that read 'Never Forget' with a picture of a floppy disk in between the words. This attire and a beard. I couldn't look any less geeky if I tried.

The next 3 years of my life passed in a blur. I got the job in the coffee shop my second-year in. It is located on Northumberland Street which is the main shopping area of Newcastle. It was run by a lovely old lady, Norma, who became like a second parent to me. I soon realised that my student financial aid would certainly not cover my love of games, films and pizza so I had no choice but to get a job. I needed something that was flexible, with somewhat decent pay that would be at least half interesting. My enthusiasm for "half interesting" was short lived but it paid the bills and supplied me with games and pizza. Oddly enough, I don't like coffee but I do love pizza. Ham and Chicken to be exact. I sometimes think that I should have gotten a job in a pizza place instead.

I finished the university, moved into a place with my Ross, Jon and Paul but kept my coffee shop job and picked up more hours. I was bored of it. I had decided to apply to GREYSOFT. Why not? Either I'll get an interview or I won't, right? Three weeks had passed since I applied to GREYSOFT and I was sitting in my room recording a "Let's Play" video for my YouTube channel of one of my favourite PC games: "7 Days to Die". I was up to day 67 on the game and I had recorded every episode. My room was the largest as I was one the pick of the rooms from a gaming tournament. It had a double bed against the back wall, a computer desk opposite which houses my PC, dual monitor display, mainly Razer accessories and my lovely comfy gaming chair which resembled a racing chair with blue stitching. On the walls and shelves were various gaming memorabilia ranging from pop vinyl figures, (Deadpool was my favourite) to posters, pictures and game collections. I didn't like to sell my games so I kept them and had some from the PS1 era up to PS2. I had then changed over to the Xbox 360 but then back to PS4. I had a nice little collection if I may say. I called this room the "Inner Sanctum". It wasn't exactly a hit with the ladies but I did manage to get one in there once. However, it was only because she got lost on the way to Hal's room one night. So, it was very short lived and with a confused young woman. My passion for gaming comes from my father who I now have not seen for a few years. He moved to Scotland once my parents divorced but he always had retro consoles on the go. Of course, they didn't seem "retro" at all to him but I had played on Atari's and so forth and had a fondness for a classic game. He is also the one that inspired my love of sci-fi, films and well basically made me the geek I am today. So, as I'm sitting there concentrating on recording "7 Days to Die", I heard a zombie sound. But not from my computer. I shook my head thinking I play too many video games as now it seemed real. But I heard it again. What the hell?? So, I grabbed my trusty club so I could make a silent kill if need be and went to turn the doorknob of my bedroom door. All of a sudden, Ross burst into my room. "What the fuck, man?! You know I'm recording!" I shouted panting in fear.

Ross threw a letter in my general direction and said in an excitingly, slightly raised voice "Look at this, man. It even has GREYSOFT printed on the front and it's addressed to you". My heart stopped. Could this be the break in life that I had been waiting for? Was it an invite to interview? Or was it a letter basically saying "Thanks but no thanks". I pressed CTRL+F9 on my keyboard to stop the recording, slipped my headphones off and picked the letter up off the floor. At this point, Jon and Paul had appeared at the door waiting expectantly to see what the letter was. I sat on the floor trembling with the letter in my hand. I was shaking so much that I couldn't even make out the words. I was holding everything or nothing in my hands. Could I even look? Ross came over to me and said, "You've got this" in a reassuring manner and I somehow managed to compose myself. But I also knew that when I had applied for GREYSOFT, I met all the essential criteria but one. They wanted someone with previous programming experience on a large scale for a AAA games company. I wondered how I could get experience working for a AAA company like GREYSOFT unless I actually worked for them. How is someone supposed to achieve this without a chance? This always annoyed me on application forms. I want to just write across the application form "Unless you employ me, how can I ever get experience you are looking for?" But I wrote down that I had helped code and create a few apps on iOS and Android and even had my own little game on PC which I was trying to get greenlit on steam and gave them a description of it and offered to send them links, etc. I was hoping it tip the balance just enough in my favour.

I got up off the floor, opened the top left drawer of my computer desk and took out a little pocket knife that I kept in there. I didn't want to risk tearing the envelope's contents, so I slid the knife carefully under flap and it cut effortlessly as it went. I turned to Paul, passed him the envelope and whispered, "Here, you read it. I won't be able to bear it if it's bad news". In passing it off to him, I hoped he would break it to me nicely if it the letter didn't contain the invite that I was hoping it would. He pulled the letter out of the envelope and he read the following:

"Dear Mr Black,

Thank you for your recent application for a programmer on our latest, yet unannounced, game creation. As you can imagine, we received many applicants." Blah, blah, blah it all seemed as Paul skimmed down the page. "Congratulations! You are one of the top applicants that we have chosen and would like to you invite you interview with us in London. The address is listed below. Please be there at 2:00 p.m. sharp on Friday, September 8th, 2017."

Paul stopped at this point as a massive smile stretched across his face and exclaimed, "Congratulations, buddy!" I could have actually hugged him! "Are you serious?", I stammered thinking that perhaps he was just teasing and trying to wind me up. He handed me the letter so I could see for myself. I skimmed through it and he wasn't joking. This was real. Ross turned to me and said, "You know what this means?? CIDER!" I didn't need to be asked twice. We headed to the shop and that night we got very drunk while I played badly at FIFA as I was way too preoccupied to concentrate on the game.

*BEEP * BEE * BEEP * BEEP * BEEP* I rolled over and I looked over at my alarm clock. It read 4:00 a.m. so I hit the snooze button, rolled back over and snuggled into my warm duvet once again. I had time. I was currently running on 3 hours of sleep. I was tired and sure I only closed my eyes 2 minutes ago but yet the night seemed long as

I was so anxious for my interview. I had tried for an early night but with the cider, the time got away from me. I closed my eyes but my mind was certainly not ready to rest. I lay there thinking of everything. What questions will I be asked? Had I left enough time for the bus journey? What would be the exact route I was taking across London? Would they like me? No scenario was left unturned. The last thing that I remember was seeing 1:00 a.m. on my alarm clock. I had taken a sleeping tablet so it was nice to see it eventually worked and I had at least 3 hours of solid sleep.

Today was the day that I was travelling to London for my job interview with GREYSOFT. This was the moment I had been waiting for all my life. As I started to nod off again, I pictured handing in my notice at the coffee shop. I even had my resignation already written out and sitting in my work locker. I didn't know if this was confidence or desperation that made me do this already. I was already thinking of the ripe smile on my face when I threw it at Stacey (my team leader) and walked out of the door for the final time letting my apron hit the floor as I did in kind of a slow motion. If I had much hair left, I would have flicked that, too, as I went. My resignation letter read:

"Dear Stacey,

This is my official notice. I hereby give one week." However, I hoped that they would just let me go straight away. If not, I may just develop a nasty cold. The letter continued, "Thank you for employing me. I will be sad to leave as I have enjoyed my time here." I mean, come on, I had to lie a little. "Thank you for all of your help and for the valuable experience that I have gained in my time here."

Yours Sincerely,

Matthew Black"

I kept it short but sweet and I didn't think it was worth writing too much as I hoped I would never be back there again. *BEEP * BEEP * BEEP* Urgh! I just hit my snooze button! Ten minutes could not have passed that quickly. "Alright, alright, I'm up. Shhhh", I said in the alarm clock's direction. I hit the alarm button to quiet the racket. Ah, silence. I thought to myself as I closed my eyes once again but just for a moment. I literally had to physically use my fingers to pry my eyes open and had to give myself a pep talk to even sit upright. Why did I do this to myself and stay up too late celebrating? I didn't even have the job yet. And after pulling that stunt, as exhausted as I was, I may have doomed myself. I was hoping that my multiple snooze alarms hadn't woken anyone else up as the last thing I wanted as to come back to tonight was to find they had trashed my room in retaliation for waking them. I rolled out of bed and made my way to the bathroom. I pulled back the shower curtain, adjusted the water temperature and climbed in hoping it would help to wake me up a bit. As the water hit my face, I started singing as I normally did in the shower. This morning's song was "Grace Kelly" by MIKA and I started trying to hit the notes. How could I guy do that? As soon as it dawned on me what I was singing, I really was hoping nobody was awake then. So, I just hummed the rest of the song for the duration of my shower. When I jumped out,

I quickly dried myself off and styled my hair. I had pretty short hair so my styles were limited but I liked to use some hair wax to push it forward and then pop up a little flick at the very front. I put on my newly purchased suit which was one of most expensive and nicest items of clothing that I've ever owned. I was wondering if I had made the right choice with such a large purchase but as I glanced in the mirror, a wave of unusual confidence came over me and I whispered to myself in the mirror, "Matthew, you look the part now so let's go knock them dead".

As someone who suffered from low self-esteem all my life, I tended to avoid mirrors as much as I could. I didn't have much confidence in school and I wasn't particularly a hit with the ladies. I had asked a few girls out but typically received a straight up "no" or "Oh, I just see you as a friend". One girl was cutting enough to look at me and say, "You're not physically attractive". I always thought of how deep words can cut and I wonder if some people even realize that. By saying so few but unkind words, they can cause enough pain to last someone a lifetime. When I started the University, I found myself online more in hopes that my personality would be able to shine through instead of my shyness and my social anxiety taking hold. I tried dating apps, joined gaming clans, chat rooms and the such in order to help me speak to girls easier. I was hoping to ultimately find myself a girlfriend. All of it was without any luck at all until one night, I logged into a chat room for teens who have social anxiety issues. It was mostly to help each other through our own experiences with social interaction. I would pop on once a month or so to catch up with people, meet the newbies and share my own stories. One night while I was logged on, a private chat window appeared from someone with the username 'funky_leashy. It read, "Hi, my name is Jennifer. I was speaking to Sam who said he was a friend of yours and said that I should hit you up as I am also attending a university and that we had pretty similar anxiety, depression and self-esteem issues so if you'd like to chat, I'm around xx". I thought about it for a bit and as usual, I wondered if it was one of my close friends winding me up. Or was this someone who genuinely wanted to speak? I responded back after a few minutes toying with various scenarios in my head. I finally settled on, "Hi Jennifer, I'm Matthew as you must know by now, ha ha! It's nice to hear from you. Sam is a lovely guy, isn't he? So, what are you studying? And at what university?" I thought I would probe a little bit to make sure it wasn't a wind up. I waited for a few minutes but it seemed like hours. Then I received my reply. "Yes, Sam is a lovely guy. We have been talking for a few weeks. He mentioned your username to me and suggested that we talk but I haven't seen you on here before tonight. I'm studying Veterinary care at Manchester Uni, how about you?" I read the response a few times. Surely this wasn't a wind up. We talked for the rest of the evening about everything and anything and we openly discussed depression and anxiety which instantly made me feel at ease. If I remember correctly, it was about 10:00 p.m. when we both logged off. A week or so passed and I kept checking the chat room to see if she was there but nothing. No emails, no messages, nothing. I started to write it off as a chance encounter never to be repeated. Of course, my anxiety doesn't help and I kept thinking she's found another guy, she was messing with me, she forgot her log in details, she was one of my friends toying with me and now all of this information will be spread around the university and I'll be humiliated. I looked at the screen one last time, took a sip of my tea, thought "Well, there's plenty more fish in the sea" and sat back in my chair. I went to click the button to log off button and as I did, *PING* I looked down a new window had opened and there was funky_leashy. I must admit I did smile and let out a small "whoop". We talked the rest of the evening, swapped numbers and pictures and within a month, we met. Things were going really well for a year or so. I would always go down to her place as she lived with just one housemate unlike me. It got me away from my busy household with Jon, Ross and Paul. She was the same age as me, 5'5" with long dark hair and of medium build (guessing a size 12) with a wicked sense of humour. But I always got the feeling that she was masking her true sadness. She was always wearing band t-shirts but that was cool as we liked the same music, the same films and even both had a fondness of chicken and ham pizza! Was this true love? Who knew but the pizza certainly helped. She became my first proper kiss, my first sexual partner and ultimately, my first heartbreak. We both got into year 3 at Uni and just saw less and less of each other. Fortnightly visits became monthly visits, a few texts a day became one a day. She suddenly stopped answering and returning my calls as much. I knew I was about to suffer my first heartbreak and I held off wanting to know or hear the truth as long as I could. Then one day, my heart was officially broken. A text popped up on my phone along the lines of this, "Hi Matthew, I know things have been tough lately. I have been so busy with Uni. I tried to make it work but I don't think I can anymore. When I finish, I am planning to move down to Cornwall to move in with my Uncle who owns a farm down there. This isn't up for any sort of discussion and I should have been honest and upfront earlier. I hope you understand my reasoning. See you around, Jennifer x" As I stood in front of the mirror in my sharp new suit, I remember laying on my bed that night for 3 hours staring at the ceiling. Should I call her? Maybe type a reply? But what could I say or do to win her back? Do I even want to try to win her back? Why would I want to try and convince someone to want me? But I loved her. I was confused and felt hopeless and lost. Not even Ross bringing me a can of cider those years ago had helped that night. I do try to still look back on that year with fondness as no matter how much sadness you feel, it's always important to know that happiness can be just around the corner. The corner may be long and winding but it can't last forever. At any moment, you can meet that certain someone who will change your life forever. Or, in my case, I was about to set off on an adventure to London for the job of my dreams. So, I straightened my tie, took one final look in the mirror, let out a deep sigh and trusted that everything happens for a reason. The universe is always watching and I believe that when we send it enough positive energy and we are clear about the path that we want for our lives and put feet to those dreams, it finds a way to make it happen. I finally rounded my corner.

Chapter III - GREYSOFT

I left the house at exactly 5:00 a.m. I knew that the bus ride was to London was going to be about 6 hours long. The time table when booking the tickets said I would be in London by 11:30 a.m. However, I had planned for 12:00 p.m. giving 30 minutes for traffic and stops. That way, I would have about 2 hours to get across London and to the GREYSOFT office for the interview. I was kind of dreading the journey. What if someone sat beside me in the waiting area and I'd be forced to make small talk? Would they want to talk to me? Would there be a major accident and I wouldn't make it there on time? So many questions were constantly going around and around in my head as I locked my apartment door behind me. I checked my pockets for the bus tickets, money and most importantly, my phone. I had about a fifteen-minute walk into the centre of town where I would climb on board the bus that would escort me to my dream.

I stepped outside and inhaled deeply. It was a crisp September morning with no one about outside. A heavy fog blanketed the air blurring the street lights and reminding me of the classic game "Silent Hill". I stepped out onto the sidewalk and as I did, I slipped my earbuds into my ears, turned Spotify on from my phone and selected my playlist I had made specifically for this journey. I had actually spent a few days on this playlist. There were 302 songs with more than a few of the usual bands. Oasis, Blur, Embrace, Supergrass, Muse, Cast just to name a few. I loved 90's music even though I was born in this decade and didn't hear much of it until after the 90's. My love for this music was thanks to my uncle who I spent most weekends with growing up. He used to take me musical gigs and was always playing some sort of 90's indie band in the car as we went places. My uncle was a lovely man though he never married. I think he saw me a little bit as a son. I spent every weekend there with him at his home. He would make me tea while we sat in front of the television waiting for the football results. We both supported Newcastle United and he always talked to me about the good old days. I had all the stripes as a child. Alan Shearer, Rob Lee, Peter Beardsley (mainly through old footage) were some of my favourite players. I wasn't into football as much these days. Not since my Uncle passed. It just wasn't the same without him. I was 17 when he passed away and he was only 43 when he was diagnosed with cancer and he passed away shortly afterward. My mam didn't take me to any of the matches. But since my Uncle passed, I found cider, pizza and gaming or the 'holy trinity' as I liked to call them. I will always remember my Uncle as the 6 foot, skinny, slightly balding man he was rather than the frail man he had become. I always thought of him when I listened to these tracks. These songs served double purpose today: to keep me company as I headed to London and to remember a wonderful man that I miss. I feel like he's nearby when I listen to these songs. But I guess I need to be honest and also state included in my playlist are some proper power ballads from the 80's to give me extra motivation and make me feel unstoppable. Such songs include "Eye of the Tiger" by Survivor. My plan is to play this song just before entering the GREYSOFT office. Also included: "Beautiful Day" by U2, "Ain't no

Mountain High Enough" by Marvin Gaye (a track from one of my favourite films 'Guardians of the Galaxy'), "Don't Stop Believing" by Journey, "I Feel Good" by James Brown , "Heroes" by David Bowie. The list went on and on. I got to the bus stop just as Oasis' "Whatever" finished playing and decided to take out my earbuds. Bad decision as I ended up pacing up and down around the bus stop. Mainly because of nerves but also it was a little colder this morning than I was expecting it to be. Plus, I need to save some cell battery so I thought I better kill the music for the time being.

The bus arrived at 5:30 a.m. on the dot. There was nobody else around which made me happy as it meant that I could choose where to sit. Most importantly, nobody would sit beside me. I showed the driver my ticket and the poor lad looked about as tired as I felt. He was probably around sixty years old and had what can only be described as a droopy face. Though he was sporting a rather fetching comb over. I looked at his name badge: "Nigel". As is normal for me in these situations I blurted out some pointless conversation starter. "It's a bit foggy out there isn't it?" Why did I choose to say that? I think even a blind person could feel the fog if they couldn't see it. Ugh. He just looked at me.
Oh god, an awkward silence! Quick! Fill it in so it's not so quiet and weird! I continued: "It's also pretty cold out there, isn't it? Brrrrr. I wish I had worn a jacket." Silence. Again. He's just staring at me now. He's judging me, I just know it. Finally, he spoke but turned away from me, "Yeah, it is a bit on both accounts". I just couldn't leave things alone and thought I'd try to end this awkward exchange

on a high note so I blurted out, "This is my first time in London. Is it nice?" Is it nice?
What sort of question was that? Why am I so awkward in these situations? Couldn't I have just made a funny quip and walked away? Nope, not me. I had to make myself sound like an idiot.
But he answered me, "It's not bad" he replied. I took this as my cue to leave and find a seat. I sat down near the back of the coach in a window seat marked 14A. I noticed there was a time table stuffed in the seat pocket in front of me so I picked it up and looked at it. It showed that we would be stopping in Durham, York and Milton Keynes. So, leaned back in my seat as much as I could and closed my eyes trying to pass the long journey ahead.

I must have dozed off as I was suddenly and rudely awakened by some woman shouting at her kids. "Here, stop running about, Cindy! Why don't you sit beside that man there and Jordan can sit beside me?"
I turned just in time to see a child no more than 10 years old throw herself on the seat beside me. Great. Now she's standing on the seat and whining. "I want to sit beside you mummy! Why can't Jordan sit beside this man?", the little girl pouted. I thought to myself "I'm right here and now thanks to you, I'm wide awake". It took a few minutes to fully come around. I looked out the window to see a sign saying 'Welcome to York'. As I rubbed my eyes and composed myself, I looked down at my shirt which now looked like it had been trodden on by a herd of elephants. But thankfully, I had my jacket to cover it. I looked down at the little girl beside me who was now thankfully sitting down but with a face of thunder and her

bottom lip quivering. "Don't worry, I'm not that bad to sit beside" I said hoping this would put her at ease. It didn't, she started crying again. I sighed and decided this would be an ideal time to start listening to music again. The rest of the journey was a nightmare. Jordan, her brother, sat behind me and kept kicking my chair. And this little girl beside me kept going between crying, fidgeting, moaning or dropping crumbs on me. Her diet of crisps, fizzy drinks and chocolate can't be good for her but they seemed to keep her quiet which was her mum's main aim I supposed. Three very long hours later, we arrived in London. I didn't particularly like kids and after that ride, I decided that maybe I would be keeping this view point. In my head, I imagined myself picking up the bag of crisps that she had dumped on the floor and crunching them up and pouring them all over her head and asking how she liked it. I quickly decided against this, brushed the crisps from my suit and made my way off of the bus.

Once off of the bus I knew I had to grab a tube to the GREYSOFT office but I had also had about two hours to kill and that journey would only take twenty minutes. I was starting to get a little hungry by now as I had skipped breakfast; however, I wasn't sure of what I wanted. All I knew was that it didn't involve crisps now. I'm sure I must be smelling of cheese and onion thanks to Jordan's fussy little sister. I wandered around for a bit and found a Greggs. Since I'm from Newcastle, this was always a Geordie's staple diet so I grabbed a sausage roll, a steak bake and, for good measure, a chocolate doughnut. "£4.50, please, love" said the woman behind the counter. "Sorry, what was that? I could have sworn you said £4.50",

I stammered. I looked down at the till and sure enough, it displayed '£4.50'. "Yes, love a sausage roll, steak bake and a doughnut total £4.50. Do you still want these items?" My jaw nearly and quite literally hit the counter but then I remembered that I was in London. I was no longer in Newcastle so I reluctantly paid and thought about adding "Would you like a pound of flesh with that, too" but I resisted the urge. I wandered on down the street towards the main road. London was INSANE! There were cars, people and noise everywhere. The air was so thick with smog. In fact, you could almost taste it. People were beeping their horns; sirens filled the air from every direction. Buses just sat there stuck in bumper to bumper traffic and filled to capacity with bored looking office workers sporting grey and black suits. This place was so far removed from Newcastle which I had always thought was a big city. But I suddenly realized how small of a fish I was in what seemed to be the world's largest pond. I kept walking towards the tube in hopes it might be a bit quieter once I got there. As I approached the entrance to the tube, I noticed a man that seemed to be about seventy years old balding but with a long, grey and straggly beard. He was sporting old dress trousers covered in stains and a wholly jumper and was maybe 5'2". He looked at me and asked, "Can you spare any change?" I decided on my normal response of looking at the floor and walking the other way. But next I knew, he grabbed my arm, "Hey, I asked you if you have any change!!?" He gripped my arm tightly and his eyes pierced right through me. I was taken back by this to say the least. What was I supposed to do now? So, I reached into my pocket and found a £1 coin and handed it to him straight away. His eyes were bloodshot and slightly creepy but he looked right into mine and said, "The end cometh tonight. If I were you, I would leave this God forsaken place". I quickly pulled my arm away and snapped, "Thanks for the info". I didn't look back but hurried down the steps into the tube station. Hindsight, I wish I had taken his advice at the time. I thought he was crazy. A nobody. I had no idea how right he was about to be.

I boarded the tube and within twenty minutes, I was at my location. I walked up the stairs of the station, turned on my Google maps and made my way to the GREYSOFT headquarters. As I approached my destination, I looked up in amazement. Here before me stood this massive glass fronted building so of course, I had to take a selfie with it in the background. I sent the picture to all my friends on WhatsApp. And when I say "all my friends", I had three and they were also my roommates. I went inside and walked up to the security desk. The man sitting behind, it looked exactly like the stereotypical security guard from every film I had ever seen. He was overweight, his shirt buttons nearly popping off, grey dishevelled hair and eating a Mars bar. Judging by the number of wrappers in the waste bin, I'm guessing it wasn't his first one today. Nor would it be his last. But I approached him, "Excuse me sir, I'm here for an interview with GREYSOFT", I said. He looked me up and down scrutinizing me then finally said, "Sign here" pointing at the sign in book. So, I did.

Name: Matthew Black

Department to see: GREYSOFT

Time in: 13:45 p.m.

Badge Number:

"Excuse me sir, what should I write in for the badge number?" He looked down at his desk and handed me a GREYSOFT lanyard with a visitors' badge number 22 on it. I looked at it like he was passing me the holy grail. I could have sworn it was shining as he passed it to me.

Badge Number 22. That's me! Badge Number 22. Wow. I have a badge number! This is happening!

I completed the sign in sheet and put the lanyard around my neck. 22 is my favourite number so this was a good sign! It had been my favourite number since I was a child. I had a teacher in primary school who I kind of fancied. I mean, obviously, my being ten years old and her being considerably older than me posed a small issue but she loved the number 22. She said it reminded her of two little ducks swimming when you wrote it with a loop and from that point forward, it became my lucky number. I think her name was Mrs. Bell. Crushes were so fickle at that age. The guard pointed towards the elevator. "It's floor 18 you that you're looking for so just head on up as they are expecting you." I walked towards the direction that he indicated and laughed at the ".....they are expecting you" line. One of my favourite franchise films of all time is James Bond. I imagined as I entered the elevator and pressed the button for floor 18, how many times a bad guy had said "Ah, Bond, I was expecting you" while stroking a cat or holding a gun in an attempt to kill our suave British agent. I looked in the mirror of the lift and repeated one of my favourite lines from Goldfinger, "Do you expect me to talk?" voiced in my mind by the greatest Bond ever, Sean Connery. "No, Mr. Bond, I expect you to die" said his nemesis. I proceeded to draw a pretend gun from under my jacket just like Bond would and "bang". The bad guy was dead. I blew over the top of my finger blowing away the pretend smoke and holstered it. I looked to my side and noticed a security camera. "OH MY GOD!" What happens if they saw that? I could only imagine the letter.

"Dear Mr Black,

We at GREYSOFT will not be employing you after studying footage of you in our elevator making some very bad James Bond impressions. Please never apply with us again."

I quickly banished that thought as I realized that I had forgotten to play my inspirational track. However, the lift was beginning to slow down so it was too late now. I looked in the mirror, practiced my best smile and made certain my jacket was fastened. "Floor 18" said a computerized ladies voice as the doors opened.

"Wow" I said out loud as I walked into the lobby. I'm inside the GREYSOFT head office. In front of me stood a giant Assassins Creed statue. I studied it and noticed that it was Ezio from the 2nd AC game. Arguably, the best one of the lot. It took part in my favourite country in the world: Italy. As the game progressed, you were able to unlock information on the areas and buildings. Whenever I'd be playing, I would sit down with Wikipedia open so I could find out more information on each building. I knew this was a bit a geeky but boy did it get me involved in the story. To the left was a room with row after row of computers set up behind a room of frosted glass and a security door. To my right was a large conference room. I could see all sorts of GREYSOFT memorabilia displayed everywhere I looked. I was in heaven. There was no way that I could even think about reducing the smile on my face. Nobody was out here to greet me, though, so I wondered what to do next. I spotted a buzzer on the security door and I decided to press it.

BUZZ

"Hello?" a voice said on the other end.

"Hi, my name is.... erm..... Matthewwwwww......" there was a few second pause. I had seemingly forgotten my surname. I finally remembered after what seemed an eternity. "Black", I continued. "Matthew Black. I'm here for the interview."

"Oh yes, thank you for coming, Matthew. Come on through and take a seat in room 1. It will be to your left as you enter"

The door opened and I took a few steps forward. I could now clearly see what was on the other side of the frosted glass. It was basically heaven. I could see endless rows of people working on what I guessed to be various games. I also noticed plenty that had beards. The lads, of course. So, I stroked mine thankful that I had kept it. I could see some of my favourite game characters too dotted around the room in various poses and sizes. Some were made of cardboard and some were life sized models made of metal and wood and some sort of ceramic substance I guessed. I could see Rayman, Desmond Miles from Assassins Creed, Aiden Pearce from Watch Dogs, Vass Montenegro, one of my favourite villains from Farcry 3, Sam Fisher from Splinter Cell and lots of tough looking army guys from various Tom Clancy games. As I stood there, I drifted into a dream state and could easily picture myself sitting at one of the desks. How amazing it must feel to look at this all day long! I knew from this point forward, that this was the job that I wanted. This is what I wanted to do.

My daydream was only broken when someone looked up from his computer screen giving me one of those 'What you looking at?' glares. I awkwardly smiled at him, quickly broke my gaze and realized that I should really find the interview room. I walked a little way down the corridor and to the right of me, I saw 'Room 1'. This is the place that I will now spend the next hour or so trying to convince someone that I was good enough to work for this company. I was so nervous. I was sweating. I was shaking. I felt sick and worse of all at this point, I realized that I hadn't used the restroom for a few hours. I took a quick look down the corridor and didn't see a restroom sign. Well, this is a problem. I tried not to think of waterfalls or the gentle sound of rain on a window. Of course, the harder I tried not to think of those things meant that it was now exactly all I could think of.

I knocked on the door to Room 1. It was a plain wooden door with a brass 1 in the middle and attached to the right of the door was a laminated piece of paper that read “Programmer Interviews”. At least this was the right place. There was no answer when I knocked so I walked in, closed the door gently behind me and chose the lone seat in front of the window. The room was I guessed maybe 10 by 10 meters. It had no game memorabilia in it and seemed to be just your typical office meeting room. There was a wooden table in the middle with some coasters dotted about and some cupboards in the back of the room. On the table was simply a jug of water and a few drinking glasses. Ugh. Water. Restroom. I tried my hardest not to look at the water. The only decoration on any of the walls was a clock that was to the left of me. It read 13:58. The ticking seemed deafening * TICK TOCK TICK TOCK* was all I could hear. I also found it a little weird how plain and dull this room was. There was nothing anywhere indicating that I was now in GREYSOFT. It was as if I could be in any office building anywhere in the world right now. It sort of shattered the illusion a little but I was snapped back to reality when the door opened. A man entered and closed the door behind him. He pulled out a chair and said, “Shall we begin?” I took a deep breath, nodded and sat forward in my chair.

Chapter IV - Strange Burgers

"Ah, sorry, Matthew. Where are my manners?" said the man. "I'm Alex, the project lead. Before we begin, do you need anything?", he asked with a slight cockney accent. I quickly surveyed Alex. He was, I guess, mid to late thirties, about 6' tall wearing glasses, dark blue jeans, a black shirt with a suit a jacket and sporting a short goatee that was slightly greying but had a shaved head which was perhaps because he was balding.

I looked at him and I thought to myself, the list could be endless: a sick bag, a toilet, a shot of whiskey to calm my nerves, something to stop this sweating. My heart was pounding so quickly that I thought I was going to pass out. My thoughts raced. Why was I here? Why didn't I just stay at home? I'm out my depth. He hates me already. These thoughts whizzed round and round in my head but I knew that I had to push them to the back of my mind.

"No", I replied as I didn't think listing any of the things circling in my head would help me. "However, would you mind if I grabbed a glass of water?" Why did I ask this? I needed the restroom already but my throat was dry and I needed the water so I wouldn't sound like a chicken trying to squawk out a reply to his questions. Alex smiled "No, not at all", he said and passed me a glass from the table in front of him. I had been reading a few articles on how to deal with interview stress and one common tip was, before answering a question, to have some water close by in case you needed some extra thinking time, just take a sip of water and delay your answer.

This, I had decided, was going to be my method; however, with how much I needed a restroom right now, maybe I should've have thought of something else. Just then there was a knock at the door. Alex looking a little annoyed said "Come in" but his eyes seemed less than impressed. An older man stood appeared wearing a suit and looking a little angry carrying a bundle of paper. "Sorry to bother you, Alex" the man said. He then looked at me for a second like he hadn't noticed me there initially. "Alex, I have some bad news which is going to knock us back a bit. Steven asked me to tell you straight away. All of our servers just went down. The general building's wife is off and the breaking news is reporting that half of London seems to be experiencing a blackout too. So, we need your advice on what to do." He said all of this without taking a breath which was impressive in itself. Alex stood up from his chair and left the room apologizing to me as he did. I must admit, I let out a huge sigh of relief and I used this time to start to control my breathing. In through the nose, out through the mouth. Slowly. On repeat. I needed to calm myself so I chose an object to concentrate on. I choose the jug of water in front of me. Again, with the water, though. Where is that restroom? I had been practicing mindfulness for a few months now to try and help with my anxiety attacks. When I felt one badly coming on like now, I learned to control my breathing, pick an object and forget about everything else apart from that object and my breathing. This would calm me down, help me regain my focus and most of the time it worked. Alex had been gone for a few minutes while I calmed myself down. I looked at my watch and it showed my heart rate at 92 which was about 30 more than normal but given my nerves, I was quite happy with that. I sat there controlling my breathing for a few more minutes and it dropped to a more reasonable 70. I now felt relaxed, a little more confident and I think I actually stopped sweating. I am so glad that this chair that I'm in isn't leather, otherwise. I would never be getting up out of it. I heard footsteps outside the door and some inaudible talking and then Alex walked back inside of the room. "Sorry about that. We seem to have some problems." He seemed quite distracted but then said, "Shall we continue?" To be honest with you I can't remember much about the interview at all. I had prepped many answers to many questions. Thankfully, everything that I had prepared myself for had come up already. We talked about games, programming, my experience, my likes, my dislikes, my strengths, my weaknesses and so on. He asked if I had any questions so I joked asking if having a beard to work here was mandatory. When I answered the final question, I remember looking at the clock and taking a deep breath. It read 14:45.

"That's it, Matthew, thank you for your time. We will be in contact with you within the next 3 working days" and with that, Alex shook my hand. I thanked him for his time, left Room 1 and walked towards the elevator. As I did, I looked into the room with the frosted glass where rows of people were before. This time, it seemed fairly empty. I couldn't imagine all of them going to dinner at the same time but maybe. I could vaguely make out that the few people that were left were just sitting there with their feet up on their desks. Seemed a bit unprofessional but also weird as it was such a hive of activity before. I heard a door close and glanced behind me to see Alex leaving the room that we were just in and head down the corridor and into yet another different room. I stood in front of the lift pressing the button to call it but the button didn't light up. So, I just stood there for a moment waiting but nothing was happening. I pressed it again and as before, nothing. I looked up at the LCD number display and that was also blank. Curious. I stood there for a couple more minutes. While waiting, I decided to pull my phone out of my pocket and turn it back so I could let my parents and friends know how the interview had gone. But as the screen powered on, I saw that I had no messages, no phone calls, no emails, nothing. I went to compose a WhatsApp group message but my phone showed that I had no signal. Strange since I'm in London and in a building that should have strong service. Then I remembered that man coming into my interview to speak to Alex. Maybe that meant that cell service was out in the area, too. I put my phone back into my pocket and I wondered what to do next since the lift was clearly not working. Beside the lift I saw a sign that said "Restrooms and stairs this way". Ah, perfect. I'm in desperate need of both if I want to move on with my day. After using the facilities, I proceeded down the stairs to the front desk where I had signed in. The security guard was standing talking to a group of people that looked quite animated. I could just make him out saying that there had been a power spike which had knocked out the servers and lifts; however, the IT crew were on their way and would have it fixed in no time. I signed out of the same book, returned my pass and I left. Outside, I found a bench to sit on. I now felt as if I could breathe again. I didn't feel sick anymore as I put my head in my hands. As I sat like this for a moment, I felt a nice cool breeze so I took off my jacket and decided to maybe dry out a little. I extended my arms out and must've resembled a large, strange looking bird for a few moments. About ten minutes passed before I felt confident enough that I was dried out and composed enough to make move about normally. Having anxiety can really suck. I sometimes thought to myself that surely it would be easier to let it win, to control me. I could sit in my house on benefits, play games all day and not have to interact with a soul. Of course, this idea has both pros and cons but I always knew I would rather be out there trying to make the most out of my life so it always nothing more than a passing thought. I decided to get my phone back out of my pocket and see if I now had service outside and luckily, I did. I proceeded to text a few people via a group text as it would be easier and faster. It read: "Hi, just wanted to let you know that the interview went well. GREYSOFT HQ was sooooooo cool! Like, it was everything I had ever imagined! I'm just going to kill some time in London so I'll be back home early morning and I'll let you know when I am back safely." After I sent this message to the intended recipients, I instantly felt less anxious just knowing that people were there to chat. It helped me feel like I wasn't alone. I opened up Google maps and wondered what I could do with my few hours in London to pass the time. I thought about being a bit of a tourist and maybe go see Buckingham Palace, the Houses of Parliament, the House Guard Parade or even just have a wonder down Oxford Street. I quickly searched 'things to do in London' and instantly regretted this decision as nearly a million suggestions appeared. London is a big place. How does anyone get anything done here? There is just so much going on. Of course, this led me to think about living here. But could I live here? I would be alone. I would have no friends nearby. I instantly closed the tab as I was starting to feel mentally exhausted at this point. With no sleep last night, I couldn't be bothered to become more anxious or to try and plan routes and work out where I wanted to go. Just ahead of me was a bar and next door to it was an internet café. I took this as a sign that I should do none of the things that Google suggested and instead go have a few drinks, procrastinate on the internet for a while and indeed kill some time. I decided that first, I would head to the pub. I could do with a nice cold pint of cider to cool me down and to hopefully settle some nerves.

The pub was one of those trendy places where you could only be employed if you were a hipster, I think. All of the guys wore skinny jeans and all beards that were neatly trimmed and not just shortened out of laziness like mine. The girls all had tattoos, varying colours of hair and wore glasses. The drinks on tap had funny names like 'Porkslap', 'Herpes', 'Wots Occurring', 'Pigs ass' and my favourite: 'Hoppy ending'. I didn't really like ale; however, I would have loved to have said to one of the barmaids, "Can I have a Hoppy Ending please?" but decided against it as they probably heard it hundreds of times and was afraid to get slapped out of annoyance. I decided to grab myself a cider instead and took a seat out back beside a window so I could watch the world go by. As I walked to my chosen seat, I noticed people were either playing board games or sitting on their iMac laptops looking relaxed and cool. I sometimes wished I could be this cool. Maybe if I moved to London, I would become a hipster. In fact, I wonder if this automatically happens when you move here? I tried to picture myself as a hipster and realized that wasn't for me. Geek it is! With cider and phone in my hand, I decided to check up on the news. The top story read: "Rolling blackouts across London. Loss of communications. Transport chaos. Flights and rail delays. More updates as we get them." I checked the routes affected and just my luck, the route that I needed to get to the bus station was out. I was going to have to take one hell of a detour to get to my bus in time. Procrastination time was nearly over before it began. I clicked on the next story that was trending and it mentioned something about scientists losing contact with a deep orbit satellite. I skimmed down through it as I was now mentally trying to plan my time and the distance to get to the bus stop on time. It was now 15:30, my bus was at 20:45 and I needed to be at the tube station by 20:15 at the absolute latest if I was going to make it there when I needed to. Because of the transport issues, I had 4 hours and 45 minutes to walk 3 miles across town. It was only a short tube ride, luckily. I even thought about walking all the way but I decided that this would be a bad idea due to the amount of walking I already had to do and my knee bothered me easily when I'd overdo any sort of exercise. So, I decided it best to order another cider and some food. I picked up the menu and, of course, you couldn't just order a normal burger. They were all called weird yet wonderful names like 'The Yuppie Burger', 'The Barack Obama', 'The Viagra', 'The Singing Cockney' and many other interesting titles. It took me longer to read the list of ingredients than anything else. I decided on 'The Burger Supreme' which was a burger with lettuce, tomato and a side of fries. Why they couldn't just call this a burger was baffling to me. Since I wasn't in too much of a hurry, by the time I finished it was nearly 17:00. I decided to drink up my third pint at this point and start the long walk to the bus station. I planned out my route using Google maps and tried to commit it to memory as my phone battery was getting pretty low. Thankfully, a few minutes ago, a nice hipster in the pub named "Bruno" lent me his charger for a few minutes as I think that he could see me panicking from my low battery. And as I walked outside of the pub, I started on my journey to the bus station. Little did I know that I was about to meet a girl named Summer and that we'd be running for our lives and that not only my day but my life as I now knew it, would be changed forever.

Chapter V - Swimming Pool

As Summer and I stood hand in hand ready to jump into the deep end of the pool, glass began to fall and debris was flying from every angle. This is it. I took one last look at Summer, closed my eyes and we jumped. Suddenly, the world went black.

I have no idea how long I was passed out but when I awoke, I was sputtering and coughing up water. I tried to open my eyes but everything seemed so hazy and blurry. I could just barely make out a figure moving away from me. "Hey, wait! Stop! Is that you leaving, Summer?" The figure stopped and turned around, I heard her voice say, "I'm sorry, Matthew" then she ran off. The world around me went black again. When I regained consciousness once again, I felt even more groggy than before and my leg felt strange. I opened my eyes slowly and brought the swimming pool into focus. The building that was previously standing was now destroyed. I managed to sit upright to try and get a better look at my surroundings. The pool was full of debris and glass was everywhere. The sky still looked as if it were on fire. I sat there for a minute taking it all in. My hearing was still off as my ears hadn't stopped ringing. I then realized that I was still in my underwear. To the left, I noticed my clothes and broken phone in a heap. This is odd as it must have been Summer's doing. But why would she do this and then run off?

I placed my hand on the back of my head. It felt wet and extremely painful. When I pulled my hand away, I saw blood. And a lot of it.

So, I picked up a piece of broken glass from the floor and tried to see the top of my head. It was covered in blood. Regrettably, I then looked down at my leg and saw my shin bone sticking through my trousers. I didn't do well at the sight of blood. My world went black once again.

"CLEAR", I heard a man's voice shouting. "CLEAR", I heard a slightly more distant voice repeat. "Hang on. We have a body over here. Bring another bag over here." Wait, was he talking about me? I'm not dead. They can't bag me. I need to somehow wake up and communicate with them. I opened my eyes but all I could see was a bright light. Was I actually dead now and didn't know it? I let out a groan. I heard a man's voice shout with authority, "FUCK ME! HE'S ALIVE! GRAB THE MED KIT! MALE. EARLY 20's. HEAD AND LEG TRAUMA. CALL FOR MEDEVAC IMMEDIATELY!" A hand touched my shoulder, "Don't worry, buddy, we'll get you out of here." My head was hurting badly now but I turned as I much as I could to look at him. He was dressed in army camouflage gear including helmet and gasmask and carrying a SA-80 assault rifle. Even badly wounded, my mind still went to video games and I recognized the gun from ZombieU and Payday 2. "Don't move, please. Help will be here shortly", he said as he poured some water from his canteen over my head to clear the wound and then gave me some to drink. "Thanks", I said, "Who are you? What happened? What did you say your name is? Where am I?" "I'm Sgt Bradford from the 1st Battalion, Irish Guards. What's your name?" "I'm Matthew, Matthew Black. I know it's a strange question but did you see a girl just run out of here? I don't think I imagined her as I saw her before the impact of whatever hit us." I'm not sure why I asked considering she had just left me to die. "No, sorry mate. We've been searching every building around here and you are the first person that we have found alive. Rest now. You'll be in a hospital soon enough", he responded in a more friendly voice. "What time is it?", I inquired. He looked at his watch, "It's 5:30". In the morning? I had been out that long? I started to feel dizzy and the last thing I heard was more shouting, a few muffled voices and then felt a needle prick my arm. Hello, darkness, my old friend. And Black goes black, yet again.

"Doctor, he's waking up", a female said that seemed close by. "Quick, grab the air", a man responded back. I felt something placed over my face. "Keep him sedated. He can't wake up yet. We need to finish cleaning and closing his injuries." My eyes began closing again. Will I ever be able to hold them open long enough to see the light of day ever again?

I lost count of how many times I had been out now. When I finally awoke, I felt like utter shit. My head was sore, my leg was sore, my body was sore. In fact, it might be easier to list what isn't sore. I think my middle toe on my right foot is ok. That's about it at the moment. When I opened my eyes, the room that I was in slowly came into vision. I was lying on what seemed to be a stretcher. To the right of me was a machine that does slow beeps when things are good. What I didn't want was the long beep. That's when things are bad. To my left was an IV drip. Above me, I could see what looked like some sort of green tent. I couldn't see much else as there was a curtain surrounding me. I felt my head and it was now covered in a bandage. My left leg was now in a heavy cast. I hoped my toes were somewhere under there as I couldn't feel a thing. I started to come around as if a switch was flicked on and all of my senses were assaulted at once. The full horror of the situation hit me.

Someone in a hurry must've run past where I was laying as my curtain moved slightly. I could then see nurses and doctors everywhere. Some were dressed in standard army issue. Some in white all wearing masks and gloves. But all were mainly covered in what looked like blood. I could see beds of injured people for miles it seemed. All my ringing ears could hear was screaming, shouting, crying. The noise was horrific. The pain and suffering that I heard was quite simply hell on earth. I imagined this is what it must be like in war. Just then a nurse walking by must've noticed that I was awake. She opened the curtain and came over to me. "Patient 387 is awake and conscious." Who was she talking to? She grabbed a clipboard from beside the IV and began to scribble on it. She looked at me, handed me a plastic cup and said, "Here, drink". It contained water, I think, as I couldn't really taste anything. She was wearing a full white overcoat and what looked like black trousers underneath. Her black hair was pulled back neatly into a ponytail. She was roughly late 40's and looked so tired and drained. She was wearing a name badge but I couldn't make it out. "NAME", she barked at me. I was a little taken back by her gruff demeanour. I must've hesitated too long. "NAME! I don't have time for this. We are a little busy here at the moment if you haven't noticed. What is your full name?" "It's Matthew Black." "Thank you. Now could you give me your full address, next of kin and date of birth?" Her tone made me feel like an inconvenience but from what I just saw through my slightly open curtain, I could only imagine the stress that she was trying her best to handle. I responded to each question. Then she just put the clipboard down and walked off. No 'thank you' or anything. So, I laid there unsure of how to feel, what to make of the situation, where I was, how I was, what happened to Summer, was this impact just in London or was it countrywide? There was no one to ask any of these questions to so I had no way to find out. I saw some tissue on a little chair beside me and decided to tear it up and place it in my ears hopes that it would drown out the noise. I pulled the heavy but very itchy cover all of the way over me up to my eyes and closed them. I needed this nightmare to be over with but I knew that this was not one that I was about to wake up from. And I was right. I couldn't sleep a wink because of the steady screams around me on top of my own pain keeping me awake. No one came to check on me for the rest of the night. I just lay there alone and frightened. I did not dare open my eyes. I kept them so tightly shut so that I wouldn't see what was out there. I apparently dozed off for a few minutes though I'm not certain exactly when. But a pretty young nurse startled me awake. By the looks of her, she was no older than me. She tapped me on the shoulder. "Hi", she said in a calm voice and checked my chart. "Hi, Matthew, my name is Jessica. I just want you to know that your vital signs are good. Your injuries are no longer deemed as serious so we will be moving you in the next 10 minutes to a recovery tent." She sounded sweet but really weird and muffled. It was at this point that I realized that I still had paper stuffed in my ears. I could only imagine what I looked like. She continued, “A porter will be here in a bit to take you. There, you will be offered tea, coffee and a meal if you feel up to it”. She smiled and touched my shoulder once again. This instantly made me feel secure as she was much nicer than the horrible woman from last night. She had one of those upside-down watches nurses always seem to have attached to their tunic. It read 12:30. She walked off and went to speak to another patient and left the curtain open so I propped myself up to have a look around. The place was a mess. Bandages and blood everywhere. Discarded surgical gloves and paper towels laid strewn about where they had tried to mop up the blood. Outside, I could hear trucks and what sounded like helicopters and airplanes. I felt like I was on the television show “M.A.S.H”. Trying to distract myself a little, I hummed the theme tune to try and drown out all this noise. I hated noise in general. I much preferred peace and quiet. Which is why I would lock myself away from the outside world for hours on end playing games. It wasn’t because I was anti-social. Well, maybe slightly, but I was comfortable on my own. I could spend many hours doing nothing and I was happy with it. I didn’t really need to surround myself with people. What I wouldn’t give right now to be sitting at home in front of my computer playing a game with a nice cold cider in hand.

I started to day dream a bit just as I heard a flat line tone coming from a machine near me.
*Beeeeeeeeeeeeeeeeeeeeeeeeeeeeeeep*The tone was long and eerie. I looked over to see a man no older than 30 laying there. He wasn’t moving. The doctors rushed over and pulled his cover off. He

was badly burned and both legs were missing. I didn't react but I couldn't stop looking, either. I just watched in slow motion as they tried to save him. I only turned away when I heard a doctor say "That's it. There's nothing more we can do". When I looked the other way, I began to cry. I didn't know what else to do. As I lay there alone, crying into the bed, I wondered if this could get any worse. The only shining light seemed to be the fact that at least I was still alive unlike that man beside me.

Just like nurse Jessica predicted, a man eventually turned up to collect me. He was dressed in full army gear wearing a mask like everyone else. He addressed himself as 'Private Wear' as he approached the bed. "So, Matthew, I'm going to take you to recovery now but first, do you want any food or anything as we will be passing the mess hall on the way?" He spoke with a slightly foreign accent that I couldn't quite pinpoint. Could I really eat anything after what I just witnessed? I decided against getting food but asked for a bottle of water instead. A nurse came over and removed the wires that linked me to the beeping machine and moved my IV drip to the wheelchair hook. Private Wear helped me up out of my cot and into the wheelchair. I looked around and from what I could quickly see, about ten people were hooked up to machines and IVs but a bit more than that had blankets covering their faces. I'm guessing they didn't make it. The nurse that just helped unhook my IV was writing out a tag and I watched her place it on the man that just passed away beside me. It said, "Deceased. Name unknown". I hope he at least had a wallet that was dropped somewhere close by or a cell phone so they could contact his family.

My thoughts were interrupted by Private Wear walking back over to me and pushing me towards the tent doors. "I would cover your eyes now, mate. It's a bit bright out there compared to in here", he said.

The doors swung open and he was right. The light was blinding and the noise deafening. I could smell something burning, petrol fumes and food all mixed in together. It was horrible and my nose was getting assaulted. As I tried to adjust to everything outdoors, two Apache helicopters thundered overhead escorting a chinook helicopter. There was activity everywhere. A loudspeaker kept echoing on repeat, "If you are injured, keep to the right. If you are fit and able, keep to the left. Women and children first". Soldiers were everywhere erecting fences, tents, guard posts, benches, portable toilets, taking care of food being and supplies being delivered. There were a few army trucks and some with medical signs on the side that were dropping off more soldiers, civilians and kits to various locations. I noticed Humvees and armoured vehicles set up in key areas offering what seemed to be overwatch to the soldiers setting up. A pair of Eurofighter Typhoon jets flew overhead directly towards central London. However, it didn't appear to be the London as I had seen before the impact of whatever it was that was causing three large plumes of smoke billowing into the sky. Where skyscrapers once stood, there was nothing. A smoky haze hovered above the city like an eerie blanket covering a dead person's face like I had seen earlier. From what I could make out, half of the Shard was missing. Bishopsgate was gone and the banking districts buildings were destroyed. I hadn't realized it but Private Wear had stopped and seemed to let me take this all in before moving me towards a bigger tent.

"I'm sure you have more than a few questions. Once you get inside, you will meet with a counsellor who will answer some things for you. Also, inside are televisions with 24-hour news coverage." He paused, "Did you have any belongings when you were found?" "Yes, I remember seeing my clothes and my cell phone in the building I was found in. I think they were brought with me but I don't know as I've not seen them." He checked my patient number and said, "Right, I'll see if I can locate your things but I can't promise anything". He wheeled me into the recovery tent which seemed nicer than the last one. The beds all had privacy curtains and the atmosphere was calm. No screaming or shouting and it helped that the staff of doctors and nurses had a calm, compassionate demeanour that was evident in the way they approached people around me. I could see televisions around showing the news but they were a bit too far away for me to see exactly what was on the screen or to hear what was being said. Private Wear wheeled me over to a desk where a young man approached. They exchanged pleasantries and this young man was handed my chart. "Ah, Mr. Black, I'm going to look after you for a few days. My name is Rob and I'm one of the counsellors here. We've reserved a space for you over in bay 30 so we're going to let you get yourself comfortable and I will be right over with a few snacks and a cup of, well, some semi-fresh tea ", he said with a comforting smile and some sort of north-eastern accent.

I was wheeled to my bay that would be my home for a few days. A nurse came over to help transfer me to the bed and then she went off to fetch some crutches for me. When she returned, she reassured me that today, I was to rest and when I felt ready, to give her a shout and she would show me how these crutches worked. I lay back in the bed still unable to process what exactly was going on in London and as I stared at the ceiling, I began to cry once again. As I lay there sniffling, my curtain opened and there stood Rob. He looked confident wearing his nicely pressed grey suit, shiny shoes, smart dark rimmed glasses and neatly cropped hair. Probably mid-twenties. He walked towards me and sat on the edge of bed placing a plate of biscuits and a cup of tea beside me on a little stand. "I'm sure you have many questions but I want you to know that I'm here to support you through this traumatic time." He paused, "There's a lot that has happened and I don't have all of the answers but I will answer all that I can." His tone was reassuring. I worried about choosing my questions carefully as I'm sure he had already been asked them a million times just today. So, I started off with what any confused person would ask, "What happened?" Not original but valid. "Details are sketchy but just after 20:00 hours two days ago, three objects hit London. One in the vicinity of the Houses of Parliament, the second about a mile from where you were found and a third near the city of London airport that seems to be smaller than the others", he explained almost rehearsed as if he had said this a few times. "What are the objects?" I asked. "We are unsure but the news is saying they are asteroids", Rob said. "So where am I now?" "You are at a safe medical zone known as Delta just off from Hampstead Heath. This was set up immediately after the incident and there are currently twenty more like it spread about as safe areas." "Do you know the number of casualties from these impacts?", my eyes welled up as I asked. "We don't know the exact numbers but BBC news is reporting over 80,000 dead. The number of injured is more at the moment but it is still very early to tell. The numbers are changing constantly are reports come in." He touched my arm and said, "Look, Matthew, I know this is a lot to take in so why don't you get some rest and we can talk more later". He gave me another one of his reassuring smiles. "I have one final question." "Go on", Rob said. "I was with a girl, Summer, do you know if she has turned up here?" He got up and walked out towards a computer on a nearby desk. He typed away for a moment then came back and said, "No, I'm sorry. Nobody has been here or is here under that name". He continued, "But communications are still very limited and prioritised towards the emergency services so I can't look at the other sites just yet. But I will. I promise". "OK, thanks, mate", I said and with that, he closed the curtain and walked away.

Over the next few days, I started to get back on my feet a bit and learned more about the incident. My roommates/friends, Ross, Paul and Jon had sorted some digs out at a friend's house and were going to meet me there in a few days. Due to the amount of injured people around, they were trying to keep the beds clear and use them for people that were badly wounded. I was beginning to recover and Rob had popped in to see me a few times during the week. It was really helpful having someone to speak to, confide in and help me try to make sense of things. It sometimes felt more like a therapy session. I kept up to date with the news and made a few friends with people around me. We would go for food together and hang out chatting away about our families, friends, what we thought actually happened, what would happen next and things like that. There's not too much fun to be had in a military base to be honest but we were safe and cared for. The base had grown massively since I first arrived. There was a constant queue of traffic coming in from NHS ambulances and police vehicles. People were being marked according to different categories and their category determined where they were moved to on base.

Category 1 = Dead
Category 2 = Serious life-threatening injuries
Category 3 = Serious but not life threatening
Category 4 = Minor injuries
Category 5 = Walking wounded
However, after the first few days, a sixth category was added to the list: Category 0 = Radiated.

Category 0 was something they were just finding out about as people within a two-mile radius were affected by radiation. But it seemed to be spreading further out. So those that weren't dead were exposed to radiation. Wait. Did that mean that I was, too? No, it couldn't be or I'd be placed elsewhere. Nobody was able to go anywhere near the objects that impacted England as they were still on fire and emitting smoke. Radiation poisoning was becoming a real thing and now a section of the base was locked down in total quarantine. I avoided that area completely. No way was I risking being exposed to that. People in hazmat suits were seen entering and leaving the building. I could only imagine how bad it was in there. I couldn't wait to get out of here, meet up with my friends and get as far away as possible from all of this chaos. Those that came in as Category 1 were instantly bagged and stored in a morgue. From what I heard, mass graves had been set up around the outskirts of the city in Watford, Epsom, Dartford and Romford. The death count was now estimated to be at 120,000 people with an estimated 300,000 injured. With army, police, ambulance, recovery, demolition and science personnel on the ground, London was becoming a very busy place. This site alone had 30,000 people either dead, injured, working or visitors at any one time. Since I was first brought to this base, it changed quickly and now high fences surrounded it, watch towers stood about containing snipers. Nobody was allowed in or out without authorization. Armed guards stood at the doors and the gates and patrolled the area. Spotlights were used at night to keep the area well lit. There was even a temporary landing strip cleaned off for small planes and helicopters. We were assured that this was for our safety but I often thought that there must be something more to all of this. Why were they going through all of this trouble over asteroids crashing here?

The communication network was mainly back up and running but about 90% of the networks were being used heavily for new, medical and military personnel so finding a cell signal or getting online was challenging. At night, it became a little easier when everyone else was sleeping so I did most of my own research then. There were conspiracy theories galore. The usual stuff like it was a government cover up of weapons testing, a crashed alien spaceship, even the Russians were getting the blame. The news carried conflicting reports. Many countries were sending supplies, people and equipment to help us out. The Red Cross was even on the ground handing out food packages and setting up shelters. Display boards were set up with missing people and recently deceased in hopes to connect with their families. These were updated daily and then posted onto a website set up by the Red Cross to collate all of the information together so people could search and find out information about their love ones. I searched for Summer on here every chance I could get but her name never appeared. Not even once. I wondered if she ever searched for me. Why did I care so much or even at all? She left me for dead.

It was now estimated that ONE MILLION people were homeless and displaced. Camps were set up in Stevenage, Chelmsford and Milton Keynes to house everyone. Buses ferried people daily to these areas where there was row after row of white tents. They were safe, fed and watered. Our government had been destroyed, the Prime Minster, Deputy PM and most of the cabinet had been wiped out in the first impact so we were now run by a type of collation government set up from surviving members of the parties but with added military, police and medical representatives actually sitting in. All had relocated to Birmingham for safety reasons.

Chapter VI - Pizza & Cider

I spent a few more days in the medi centre recovering before being released. London was still mainly a no-go area and roughly 200,000 people were now dead and countless more were missing. A one-week period of national mourning had just ended and I had now moved to a house which Ross, Jon and Paul had set up for me. One of the military men gave me a ride. I must admit, this was so much more comfortable and I was glad to be away from the militarized area. I was still technically within the London area but it all seemed so distant. I was recovering well. The UK was getting back on its feet and life was somewhat returning to normal outside of London. Donations had been pouring in from all over the world. The crowd funding page stood at a massive £2billion with the rest of the world's governments planning billions of dollars in aid packages, too.

We still knew very little about the actual incident. All that was still being released to the public is that three objects struck London, what the death count was at the moment and that many people were now living in camp. The lack of news was concerning. We were not told what "areas" were too dangerous nor where the radiation was too strong. Some people had managed to grab grainy shots of the objects. Others reported seeing helicopters circling above the objects and seeing people actually entering the objects but very little of this could be confirmed by any hard evidence. There was a media blackout on reporting what the objects might be which simply strengthened most people's theories that these objects were something not of this world.

I spent the next week or so recovering in my little safe place. My family was due to pick me up in a few days. Jon, Paul and Ross were staying down the road in a hotel. They met a few people down here who unfortunately were now missing so they were trying to help support their families in any way they could. I was still in a cast but preparing to head back up home with my family once they arrived. To be honest, I hadn't had much time to myself and I wasn't about to, either. I missed my quiet time. My alone time. I kept thinking about Summer and what might have happened to her. She had such a lovely face and smile. Every time I thought of her, my heart skipped a beat. But why? She left me to die. I'm not sure I'll ever get over that. Who does that? I was still in shock. My depression and anxiety were off the charts and I just wanted to go back home, relax and try and move on with my life. I did worry that I would be back serving coffee in a few weeks and of working at GREYSOFT. A shudder ran down my back at the thought.

It was Monday evening and Ross came to pick me up to go have pizza with the crew. They ordered my favourite pizza for me: ham, chicken and cheese. As I was sitting with Ross and Paul in their hotel room, we had the news on in the background. The same stories seemed to be running: thousands more dead, aid flooding in, emergency numbers to contact and so on. The news had pretty much become a 24/7 never ending roll of despair. It was now four weeks after the incident, slightly less time was getting dedicated to this as "local news" was starting to creep back in. The news man cleared his throat, "Police are asking for your help after a local woman of Victoria Street went missing last night. She is thirty years of age last seen last evening climbing into bed next to her husband. He woke up this morning to find her missing. Please carefully view the photo displayed on screen now and contact your local police at 101 if you have any more information on her." Unbeknownst to us, in the background of this very news story was the start of one of the greatest threats that humanity has ever faced and, what is now referred to as Wave 1, had just started.

"Turn that shit off", Ross shouted and I flicked the television over to the PS4 channel. We fired up a game of FIFA while eating our pizza. Just like old times. Sort of. Paul went next door to grab Jon so we could have a two on two game while we waited for Jon's new friend, Chris, to return with a few boxes of cider. Chris had picked the short straw so he had to go out into the rain to the shop to grab cider. His pizza was going cold but we soon made sure that it was demolished as it seemed such a waste. The night continued pretty uneventfully. Well, apart from Chris coming back absolutely drenched and throwing an empty pizza box at me when he realized there was no pizza left. I don't think the comment of "You snooze, you lose" went down very well. To be honest, it was a dick move.

I decided to sleep on the sofa bed in Ross's room as the weather was still horrible and too much alcohol combined with a leg cast seemed a disaster waiting to happen. I was out in a blink. The sunlight pouring through the window woke me. I looked at my phone: 10:30 a.m. Wow! I'd not slept that much or that soundly in ages. Ross was still zoned out as I could hear him snoring. I quietly turned on the little television in his room but the news said nothing new. So, I decided to look for articles online. The first one read "Police receive widespread reports of missing people. So far, twenty-five people from different parts of London have gone missing. Further news as we receive updates." I logged onto Twitter as it had become my go to place for news. Typically, information not shared with the public could be seen as it was the public posting it. Pictures, videos, different viewpoints were all available and pretty quickly at that. I checked the trending stories and found one in with 1,167 retweets. I opened it and started scrolling down through the comments. Unfortunately, missing people had become common place now. It was estimated that 50,000 people were now "officially missing" but these were basically those presumed dead at the impact sites. London was covered in missing posters, banners and countless families combed the streets and demolished buildings searching for their loved ones. But THESE missing people were different. They didn't go missing until last night. Like they were snatched while sleeping. No noise was heard, no entry point was visible, no clues at all. They just vanished. Their names, ages and pictures started trending now and where they had been last seen, I'm guessing:

Leslie Wolfe – 27, Asleep next to husband
Katelyn Key – 12, Asleep in room
Eve Masterson – 12, Asleep at friend's house
Norah Stroud – 67, Asleep next to wife

Robin Ibbott – 45, Missing from a police cell
Michayla Niemeck – 37, Missing from home
Theanna Jeffers – 19, Missing from hotel room

The list was endless. There were tourists, locals, people in hotels even people in police custody. All just vanished. It was random, unnerving and police were baffled. They were going to issue a statement at noon. I was glued to this story and could not stop scrolling. They even provided a number to call if anyone had any information at all. Just then, there was a loud bang on the bedroom door. I nearly hit the ceiling having been in such deep concentration.

"What the fuck?", Ross grumbled as he was awakened from the loud noise. There was another loud bang at the door. "Guys, open the door now! It's Chris", came the panicked voice from the other side of the door. I quickly got up and opened it for him. Chris came rushing inside and ran directly into the sofa bed before stopping. His face was as white as a sheet and there is, he stood in his boxers looking absolutely frightened. Ross roller over on his side so he could see Chris and asked again, "What the fuck do you want, Chris?" But Chris just stood there speechless like he was traumatized or something. It was very odd. Was he sleepwalking? "CHRIS!!", Ross shouted this time with a bit of anger in his voice. At this point, Paul came rushing through the door. "Guys, get your clothes on now. Jon is gone!", Paul shouted. "What do you mean 'gone'?" Ross asked. "He was here last night when we all went to bed but when we woke up this morning, he wasn't on the couch.

And he wasn't in the bathroom so we searched all over inside this hotel and outside of it and he is nowhere to be found", said Paul. "FUCK!", I screamed aloud. Could this be linked to the other disappearances? Is Jon's name about to be added to the list of missing people? I decided to keep those thoughts to myself at the moment in case he had just gone for a walk or something. Chris continued, "His phone, keys and wallet are all still on the stand beside the couch." Ross was quickly getting dressed and so was I. We decided to split up. Ross was going to check every area outside of the hotel and Chris was going to speak to reception to see if they had seen anyone matching his description leave during the night or early morning. Paul was just going to wait in our room in case Jon showed back up and I was going to check floor by floor for him knocking on every single door. After about an hour, we all returned to our hotel room. Jon was nowhere to be found.

At this point, I decided to tell them all what I just read online. I opened BBC news and said "Hey, guys, you may want to see this." I held my phone out and showed them the latest news story that I had read. All at once, the colour drained from their faces and an eerie silence filled the room. We just stared at each other saying nothing. None of us wanted to believe that Jon had gone missing but we were all thinking it and we knew but none of us would accept it. None of us said a word. Ross went back outside and Paul, Chris and myself went our separate ways once again and continued looking for him even though we had just checked out every possible avenue. Six hours had passed and there was no sign of him anywhere. We all arrived back in the hotel room and flipped on the television. We saw that the breaking news updated to saying 49 people were now known to have gone missing. We decided to call the police as we were finally resigning to the fact our friend might be one of the missing. Before doing anything, though, we thought it best to talk to his mam first. Unfortunately, Ross drew the short straw on this one. I'd have rather gone to buy cider in a rainstorm 500 times and come back every time to no pizza left for me than to make this phone call. Ross explained what had happened and all I could hear on the other end was a voice wailing, "No! NOOOOOO! Not my Jonny!" Ross even started to cry. We knew, given her anguish that she had not heard from him, either.

I picked up my cell and decided to phone the helpline on screen. "Hello, missing persons hotline, how can I help you?", said a far too cheery lady's voice on the other end. I was oddly the least shaken of the group so I decided to do the speaking, "Yes, I think my friend has gone missing", I said.
Her tone dropped as she replied, "OK, please tell me what's happened, dear". I explained what had happened, the time scale and answered the rest of her questions as best as I could. She told me that someone would be in touch with me soon. When I got off of the phone, we all just sat in silence for a good hour or more. None of us were sure what to do or say. What do you even say in a time like this? I mean what is even going on? How can people just vanish? Is it linked to these asteroids? Where have these people gone? Where was Jon? My jumbled up messy mind was all over the place. I started to think about the past few days. WHAT THE FUCK was going on? How could I go from living my dream heading to an

interview in London to THIS? My best friend gone? People dead? London in ruins? My head was spinning, I started to breath erratically, my vision blurred then blackness.

"Matthew, Matthew", I heard someone in what seemed like a distant almost heavenly voice and then I felt an arm shaking me. "Come on, Matthew, wake up", I started to open my eyes and I could see Ross standing over me. "You passed out! Are you ok, dude?!""Yeah I think so", I said, "Not sure what happened there but I'm ok". He passed me some water and I took a sip as he helped me up and onto the edge of the couch. I suddenly heard 'The Chain' by Fleetwood Mac playing and I realized that it was coming from my phone. I looked down at the screen and it was my mam. We spoke for a while and I reassured her that I was ok and was as the hotel with my friends. I didn't dare tell her about Jon just yet as she'd just worry more about me than she already was. While I was on with her, everyone else decided to call their families, too. It had been a long, emotionally taxing day so we all decided to head to bed and call it day and try to sleep this nightmare away.

Chapter VII - REM

Morning came and none of us had slept a wink, really. We all eventually wound up crashing in the living room hoping to catch the least bit of news about Jon. Cans of Red Bull and Monster were everywhere as we tried to keep watch of the news all night long but we heard nothing new. I wandered over to the wall mirror and looked at myself. Did I look as badly as I felt? Uh, yeah, I sure did. My eyes were bloodshot, my head was hurting and I felt like utter shit. I put my head in my hands and stood there for what seemed like a month. I looked over at Ross, Paul and Chris who looked equally as bad as me but that's not surprising with how little we had slept. What we didn't know at this point is that we had just managed to survive Wave 3.

The BBC news was reporting that there was going to be a press conference at 10:00 a.m. live from Birmingham from the new Joint United Kingdom Government, as they were called, and that NO further news would be broadcast until this time. We all just kind of sat there in silence again flicking through the channels and no news at all anywhere. I walked over to the window to look out onto the street below and could see a long convey of army trucks heading north. In between every fifth army truck, there was tank and an armoured personnel carrier. Helicopters and airplanes flew above. I opened the window to let some air in but also to get a better look at what was going by below. Ross ran over to the window, "What the fuck is that?" For some reason, I simply pointed down below at the noise without speaking. I wondered if they just withdrawing from the area or setting up a new camp nearby. Maybe operations are being moved outside of London. We were all at the window peering out at this point watching until everything was out of view. What do we do now? We always knew how to come together as friends and tackle any situation but not this one.

I cleared my throat and as I did, everyone looked at me, "Guys, I know we said we would be checking out tomorrow but I really think that we should get the hell out of dodge as quickly as possible. I know Jon is missing and I know we want to find him. We need to get the fuck out of this shit hole, away from this mess and back home with family. We can't stay here any longer. It feels dangerous and something isn't right." I paused here to take in the room, everyone seemed to be nodding. " I think we should just get packed, get to the train station and just get home. Let the police do their job and look for Jon. They'll contact us if they find anything." I put my arms around Paul and Ross and pulled them in close to me and said, "Come on, you know we need to get out of here." There was very little discussion between us. We knew Jon's family was on their way down after hearing the news and they were going to the police in person. I needed to stop by the Buxton's house that I had been staying at for a week or so to gather up my things so I asked Ross to give me a ride back and we all agreed to meet at the train station in an hour to head home. I was just hoping my mam wouldn't set off early to come get me when I would be heading back up home so I called her and left her a voicemail hoping she'd hear it in time. I hobbled outside on my crutches and climbed into Ross's truck. It was only a short ride back; however, it would have taken me a while to walk it. In about twenty minutes, I was all packed and ready to go. As we pulled up to the station, I noticed Chris and Paul standing waiting for us. Already, it was 11:50 a.m. They were looking at a large display screen with about roughly seventy other people. On the screen was a ten-minute countdown timer displayed over what I could see as a small room containing a table with three microphones on it and behind those microphones were three chairs. Standing off to the side of the table was a UK flag and a UN flag which seemed like an odd choice but they had been sending a lot of aid our way recently.

Ross and I got out of the truck and headed over to them. I looked up at the arrival board and noticed a train to Newcastle was due in twenty minutes. Since the incident, the rail network had been pushed to max capacity. Trains were almost constant so the board was full of trains almost every few minutes going in every direction. Because of this, at least I knew that I would hopefully be home within the next few hours. I stood with my friends and looked up at the screen. The countdown now said 4:55, then 4:54, 4:53, 4:52, 4:51 it was mesmerising to watch. As it counted down to zero, the numbers faded and you could see the room filling up with journalists. A "LIVE from undisclosed location" appeared along the bottom of the screen and the subtitles read: "These are live pictures. We CANNOT tell you where these photos are being beamed from but please stand by".

A door to the left of the table opened. First through was a man in UK military uniform. He was covered in medals looking highly important and holding a black file in his left hand. His name flashed on the bottom of the screen "BRIGADIER Andrew Whitehouse (Special Recon Unit)". He sat down to the right-hand side of the table. Following him was a lady looking rather smart but was tall and imposing. She took a seat to the left and as she did, her details flashed up on screen "Janet Anderson (Director of NASA a special envoy, working in partnership with the UK space Agency)". Finally, following her was another man dressed in a smart suit and as the subtitles displayed "Richard Evans (Head Communication Officer for the Joint UK Government)". He sat in the middle of them both, glanced around the room quickly then started speaking. At this point, the subtitles began to scroll across the bottom of the screen without breaking: "My name is Richard Evans. I am reading a prepared statement by the Joint UK government. This conference will be streamed worldwide and all other countries have prepared their own response. I am also joined by Brigadier Whitehouse and Miss Anderson who will also be adding to this statement. There will be NO questions at the end and I cannot stress enough that what we are about to tell you, will need to be dealt with and responded to as best we can as a joint world effort". He took a sip of his water and the camera zoomed in on his hand which visually shaking. "I will now read the statement:

"On the 15th of July at 8:23 p.m., three objects entered Earth's atmosphere and struck London. We suffered major loss of life and billions of pounds of damage but the efforts of our emergency services and partners were unparalleled. Everyone's dedication and strength since this time has been a true inspiration. I know a lot of frustration has come from the lack of information regarding what happened but until we knew the true nature of what we were dealing with, we could not give out any information. This has now changed and all of the information that we have will now be divulged to you. I will now hand you off to Miss Anderson who will explain further."

"Good afternoon, everyone", she had a very strong, southern American accent. Following her greeting, two objects appeared on screen circling the Earth. "What you are seeing here are the two objects that struck our planet. They had actually been spotted about two months ago and we have been tracking them ever since." The image changed to a closer photo taken from a satellite showing that the objects were actually not asteroids at all but some sort of metallic object. "We at NASA shared this information with every worldwide space agency so that we could keep track of and monitor the objects. They were given code names X129 and X130. For two months, there was very little movement. They seemed to be in some sort of holding pattern at a distance just beyond the moon's orbit. From what we could tell from these images, the objects looked solid but did have a few fault lines in key areas which we were unsure what they were used for. We decided to try communicating using radio waves which didn't work at all. Then our colleagues at the Russian Space Agency, disguised a weather satellite launch and sent a probe up to investigate." Another visual graphic showed up on screen of the probe approaching the object but it immediately vanished. "As you can see from this graphic, the probe was unsuccessful as far as we could tell. It closed within twenty kilometres and then it vanished. A large heat source was detected just before they lost contact. This was taken just three days before the objects hit London. I will now hand you back to Mr. Evans", she sat back in her chair looking nervous.

The graphics disappeared and the camera was now zoomed on Mr. Evan's face. I could hear whispers from the crowd around me but a few had grabbed their luggage and were running off. But basically, all of London seemed silent. I guessed that everyone was probably glued to the press conference like us.

"Thank you for that, Janet. At this point, we realised that this object was not as innocent as we first thought. That was further demonstrated when, and I'm very sad and sorry to announce, the International space station was destroyed with the loss of four lives from the USA, UK, Mexico and Russia. This tragedy took place the day before the objects hit us. All of the information that you are hearing right now was classified as top secret up until this moment. Presently and furthermore, these objects are noted as a threat. They are no longer something intriguing that NASA discovered and that worldwide space agencies were monitoring. This is now being made known to all world leaders that we believe this to be an attack and are taking active military manoeuvres. We were unable to track or forecast where these objects would land but as we now know, they targeted London for unknown reasons. Given that our best intelligence agencies could not monitor their motives or time or location of planned impact, we thought it only fair to give you, the public, an honest answer. We are still trying to ascertain their motive and communicate with them in order to resolve this situation. To date, this has been an unsuccessful endeavour. I will now pass you to Brigadier Whitehouse who will update you further. Thank you."

I looked around me at the looks of panic on people's faces. It was intense to say the least. I heard a woman scream, people were crying, more people were running away, several were trying to hail taxis causing traffic to back up, everyone was trying to get away to somewhere. I looked at the board, my train was only five minutes away. I only had to wait five minutes more to go home. I turned to Ross, "Can you believe this? It's unreal. isn't it?" He just nodded at me. I looked at Paul and Chris and both of them had the same similar, confused, scared expressions on their faces. I stood there and thought you know what this sounded like? A game intro. One of those classics like "only you can save the world" as you climbed in your eight-bit spaceship to do battle. Or maybe like the film "Arrival". I wondered if we had scientists aboard these ships trying to talk to whatever these things were aboard them. I quickly decided that I was hoping this entire event was more like "Arrival" where they shared technology with us. I didn't want to live out the film "Independence Day" where they aliens wanted to wipe us out. However, for a change this was in ENGLAND not New York. I'd always wondered if our British signals ever reached into space as most everything seemed to happen in New York. I guess I have my answer now.

My thoughts were interrupted by the booming military voice of Brigadier Whitehouse. “Ladies and Gentlemen, I will be announcing a series of military measures following this new information and will let you know quickly what we have been doing on the ground. First off, I just want to say thank you for all of the support and tolerance that you have shown to us over the past few weeks. I know many of you have been involved personally. We have been trying to communicate with the objects for several days via different methods. We had some of the top UK and world scientists trying to set up different communication lines. We were achieving nothing until two days ago at 11:00 p.m. We received a pulse signal from one of the objects and our scientists managed to decode a very small message and it read,” a graphic flashed up on the screen, “Humans, we will take you until there are no more.”

He continued, “This message was received and decrypted within a few hours. That night, as you are aware, about fifty people went missing from various areas around London. Last night, the same message was received and it’s with great sadness that we estimate about five hundred people have gone missing”. He paused at this point and took a sip of water. “What in the actual fuck?”, I heard Ross say before the Brigadier’s voice started again. “This hostile activity cannot continue. We are currently receiving units from all NATO members to contain this situation. Unfortunately, this is where I now announce the following measures and this comes from the highest position and is out of our hands.” A graphic appeared on the screen with the following text, the general read:

"1 – Martial Law has now been imposed across the London area", a map appeared and showed basically the area within the M25 circular road.
"2 - No public transport will operate outside of this area as of 12pm today", I looked to the board beside the screen and EVERYTHING was cancelled.
"3 – The Army, Navy and Air force in conjunction with other countries have set up checkpoints, patrol areas and are forwarding operating bases to the outside of the M25."
"4 - To contain the threat to the London area, NOBODY will be allowed IN or OUT beyond the M25 after noon today. If you are inside this zone, stay indoors, lock your doors and stay away from military personnel. Do not go near the foreign objects and do not in any way interfere with military operations. A curfew of 7:00 p.m. through 7:00 a.m. is now in force. I have to stress that until we ascertain the threat level, if you do try and leave the area, then it will have consequences."
"5- The final measure is that until we know how to stop the objects from issuing threats, all communication lines will also be cut at the hours just specified previously." He closed with the following words, "Good luck and God bless London. We certainly need it."

Massive panic immediately ensued. Everyone around us started running though I wasn't certain where to. Chaos filled the air between screams and car horns. London was now gridlocked. Jets and helicopters flew overhead. Ross grabbed me and pulled me to the side just as a motorbike sped in my direction. I glanced up at the screen that we were just watching and it was all black but for a single message: 'God help us all.'

Chapter VIII - Districts

Just over a year passed since that fateful day that the words "God help us all" were forever burned into my brain. Most people now measured the days by 'waves'. We are now living in wave 378. "Wave" is the term given to the evening abductions. Each night, at roughly the same time, within the no go zone of London, a number of people vanished varying from fifty in wave 1 to a maximum of 10,000 during wave 15. Records stopped being kept after that so current and accurate numbers are not known. Each evening is a new wave. Each evening, friends, loved ones and family members vanish without a trace. It was seemingly random and scientists all over the world to date hadn't found any way to stop it. If you closed your eyes and had someone next to you, there's a good chance that would be gone when you opened your eyes. Nobody was ever found again after they disappeared. Nobody has ever returned. The number of reported cases outside of the LNGZ (or as most people called it the "fucked zone"), was minimal. Obtaining news from the outside world was never easy but the number stood at 1,000 outside London of people that disappeared whereas inside the zone, it stood at an estimated 1 MILLION. Those who had not made it out of London in the few hours that we were given were stuck here. The world treated us like some sort of incurable cancer. Yes, they provided aid and tried to give us assistance from afar but on the whole, they just fenced us off in hopes the problem stayed one area without spreading further hoping it would just all go away. rea. A high metal fence was installed along London's parameter and guard posts were erected about every 1 mile. Somewhere around wave 200, the army demolished the road with explosives and turned it into a DMZ. Calling this once thriving city a war zone was an understatement. The only route in and out was where the old M1 meets the M25. In this vicinity, there stood an electric gate about twenty feet high covering two lanes of the road. Black and yellow warning stripes covered the gate and at the top was a sign stating" STAY BACK – DO NOT APPROACH THIS GATE – LIVE FIRE WILL BE PERMITTED". Guard posts were on either side, barbed wire, tanks, mounted guns and soldiers protected the entrance, large flood lights lit the area and loudspeakers would relay instructions to those leaving and entering.

Since the press conference announced martial law a little over a year ago, people went crazy demolishing and looting anything that was left standing, mass protests swept the capital, buildings were set on fire, military convoys were attacked. A few world leaders protested our treatment of the situation but on the whole, most agreed that until the threat to the world had been assessed then this was the only course of action. Unfortunately, we as well as many other millions of people in London were stuck here. We tried to escape but we couldn't. The scale of the traffic and clusters of people was just too much. That's not to say that we didn't try but the military patrols always found us and pushed us back into London. Communications and electricity were sporadic at best. I still managed to speak to my family every night but it just depended if we could catch each other at the right time. London started to resemble some sort of nineties film like "Escape from L.A". It was like we were now living in a city of the damned with three giant alien spaceships that crashed in the centre of us. Violence, gun and knife crimes escalated against each other. People were trapped like animals and they were starting to act like it. Emergency services became stretched so thin and after a few months, London was basically no more. It was now divided into districts. Social standing and money talked now and the difference between have and have nots started to really show. On top of this, people had started to become nocturnal. It seemed to be the only way not to be taken in the night was to STAY AWAKE. People started to sleep all day and stay awake all night long. The phrase "You snooze, you lose" really had new meaning.

The newly formed districts were named as follows:

District X – Crash Site One – No go area

District Y – Crash Site Two – No go area

District Z – A three-mile radius out from the centre of Westminster. This is where all the military and scientists were stationed and was still within the extreme danger zone as the army regularly bombed, shot at and generally tried to destroy the objects to no avail.

The rest of London was split up into roughly twenty districts which sort of resembled a dart board the way that they were laid out. However, in numerical order, the north east point around Hayes being District 1 and then running east and round like a clock.

Districts 3, 4, 5 and 6 were designed as refugee zones. This is where the large camps had started to spring up once the gates were shut and hundreds of thousands of people ended up living. It was generally safe, well protected, tended to by the Red Cross and overall not a bad place to be. However once in, any sort of traveling about was severely limited.

Districts 15, 16, 17 and 18 were to the south west of London. This is where the wealthy had taken up roots. Large areas had been cleared and they were protected by the army and private security. They had an endless supply of power, communications and had started construction on gated communities. They knocked down homes, buildings and businesses to clear areas for them to live. They had set up large flood lights in most areas so it resembled having daylight 24/7. For this reason, we called these districts the "light zones".

Districts 1, 2, 7, 8, 9, 10, 11, 12, 13, 14, 19 and 20 were for the rest of us who didn't want to be in a refugee area or weren't rich enough to set up elsewhere. These areas were rough to say the least. Rolling blackouts, looting not to mention dangerous. Murders, muggings and violence occurred daily. These were not places that you wanted to be during the day. Many supplies from the army had been stolen so guns were also common place now, too. Some of these districts were slightly better than others with residents patrolling the streets trying to keep the streets safe. All of these districts were known as "dark zones". The military didn't enter so there was little law and order. Not every part of the dark zones were bad, though. There were pubs, plenty of places to rest and access to fresh food and water but if you had the money. Money didn't quite hold the same value as it used to. Most things could be bought from markets or local traders pretty easily and I mean ANYTHING from bread to guns and unfortunately, people. Scum in these areas were kidnapping and then selling young girls and women to passers-by to make a quick quid. London was now pretty much a living nightmare.

Chris, Paul, Ross and myself set up home in the Buxton's old house. Somehow, they had made it out of London. We think they did anyway as we never heard from or saw them again. Their home was situated in what was now called District 19 and was very close to one of the light zones so it was relatively safe. We were able to grab supplies and see friends during the day and at night we were relatively safe from the humans but the alien threat still stood. People lived their lives like every day was their last now. Being so close to the light zone also had other benefits as we were on the same grid so electricity was pretty consistent and we usually had phone signal and a stable internet connection. We did have to do some decorating to the house meaning for protection. So, the windows were boarded up and extra locks were installed. We didn't have any guns but we had some fierce cricket bats which we found in the garden that we kept close by at all times. We would joke that were living a scene from "Shaun of the Dead" when the zombie first turns up and they run outside hitting the zombie to the tune of "Don't Stop Me Now" by Queen. If one of those aliens ever showed up, that's just the scene we'd be living for real. We've had some good times in our house but unfortunately, tragedy was never far away. Only a year had passed but we were not all together any longer.

Chris was taken in wave 200. We were having an all-night session as normal trying to stay awake. He had managed to find girl a few waves earlier who lived a few streets down and invited her back to our place. Unfortunately, he made the terrible mistake of smoking some cannabis with her. It wasn't uncommon as people resorted to drugs to help get through what was happening. But this decision made him far too relaxed which knocked him out cold and by morning, he was gone! His disappearance hit the group hard. We had managed to go 200 waves living pretty normally but this was the change we always hoped wouldn't come.

Paul was taken in wave 230. He was becoming more and more depressed after Chris vanished and was sick of just sleeping his days away. He was becoming increasingly unstable and had actually tried buying a pistol so he could kill himself. He decided that enough was enough and started sleeping whenever he wanted. He managed to survive 10 waves before he was taken.

Then it was down to only Ross and myself. But we met a young lad, "Tom" and his crazy uncle "Nigel", they lived in a house just down the street which had been raided and set on fire. Since they no longer had a home, we asked them if they wanted to move in with us. Tom was a little younger than us at 15 years of age. About 5' 10", skinny, always wearing skinny jeans and a band t shirt, short spiky dark hair, an earring in his right ear and an eyebrow stud above his left eye. He had been kicked out of his home when he was 14 after telling his parents that he was gay and then he moved from Southampton to London to start living with his uncle. We all got along on pretty well. Tom was pretty much a geek like Ross and I and he chipped in around the place and helped with getting supplies. His uncle was as mad as a box of frogs. He claimed to have spoken to the aliens and he always believed they would attack Earth. He was always speaking about government conspiracies and lizard people. He used to smoke A LOT of weed when he was younger and I always wondered if there was a connection. Nigel was 55 years of age, grey unruly hair, bushy grey beard, overweight and covered in tattoos. Some of his tattoos were awful and I wondered if he got some when he was high. For all of his madness, though, he was a great uncle to Tom and looked after him and took him in and gave him love and security when Tom needed it most. Nigel also had a stash of army weapons that he bought from some bloke down in the market and had plenty of supplies so they were a much-welcomed addition in helping Ross and I survive.

We cohabited well for a while but as always in this hell, things didn't run smoothly for very long and during wave 310, things went from bad to worse. We were sitting in the house, Nigel on guard duty and Tom and I smashing some two player FIFA. There was a loud bang and a round of gunfire ricocheted off of the wall behind us. "GET DOWN", I shouted. Ross came running downstairs just as heard more gunshots. This time, Nigel was firing back with a classic SA-80 Assault rifle used by the British Army. "There are three of them", he shouted over the noise. "Two are in front of the wall out front and the other has gone around the side. I can't see him anymore but it looks like they are all armed." Tom jumped from the sofa, grabbed a pistol and moved towards the rear of the house to cover if someone tried to get in. I hid lying flat on the sofa with no idea what to do. I had not been interested in learning how to use a gun but Tom had been well trained by his uncle. More rounds pelted inside the house. One hit the television, one hit near the sofa that I was one and another barely missed Nigel by a few inches. Just then, the side living room window board came off. When I looked towards the commotion, I could see the barrel of a gun pointing at us. The room lit up with gunfire and everything seemed to be in slow motion. I saw Tom run in as he unloaded five to six rounds into the direction of the window. Nigel, who had been watching out of the front windows, spun around targeted the same living room window as Tom. "We got the bastard", Tom said as he ran to the window and peered out. "He's on the ground bleeding out! What should we do?" Nigel ran over to the window and unloaded another round into the man on the ground. "That's it. He is certainly dead now", he grunted. "And would you look at that! His mates have run off and left him for dead." Nigel ripped open the living room door, ran outside and sent a few rounds of gunfire down the street after them. It wasn't until this moment that I realized that I'd not seen Ross move at all. I turned around and saw Ross slumped onto the floor. I ran over to him, rolled him over and tried to shake him awake. "Ross! Ross! Can you hear me?!!" Then I noticed an entry wound through his left temple with an exit out the other side. I was instantly sick. I cried over his broken, limp body. He had been my friend for so many years and now, just like the rest of them, he was gone. That moment changed me forever. Burying my best friend in an unmarked grave was a harrowing experience.

Shortly after this horrific day, Nigel, Tom and I decided that we would no longer stay put and instead needed to be mobile. We acquired the "Beast" when looking for some supplies in District 17. We walked past an abandoned prison area and inside was a brand new, half sprayed and logoed up G4S prison transport van just sitting there. We took a closer look and found the keys in the back office and decided this was for us. What more could we want? It was secure and most likely bulletproof. There were compartments in the back for storage, guns and areas in the back that we could use as rooms where the prisoners would usually sit. We didn't modify it at all apart from a ram at the front which Nigel fitted for the countless roadblocks and debris littering the streets. I am never sure why Nigel used mattresses He seemed to have a fascination with using mattresses as protection on everything. When I asked him why as they are so soft and flimsy and not at all bullet proof, he just said that it stopped the alien signals and they couldn't find your or get inside your head. And since I had no idea what else might stop that from happening, who was I to argue with the crazy old coot. That evening passed and we determined that we had just survived wave 379. Maybe the mattresses helped hide us from the aliens after all.

Chapter IX - The Beast

It was a cold and windy night as I glanced at the LED display reading 01:09 a.m. We were somewhere inside of District 8 and had been driving for a few hours now. One of the rolling blackouts hit one of the dark zones so tensions were very high. We approached yet another blockade in the road "Shall we just smash through it?", Nigel asked.

I didn't even have time to respond before I heard the revs climb. Nigel dropped a gear and Tom and I braced for impact. There was an almighty crash as the Beast made impact with the burning wooden barrier in front of us. Wood and tires went flying. I was thrown forward and then immediately backwards violently. There was a loud crack as a brick was thrown at the protected windshield followed by another and another. The revs climbed once again as we cleared the blockade and powered on down the street before veering sharply left towards District 7. "Well, that was a bumpy ride", I half joked trying to lighten the mood. I instructed Nigel to drive to the next turning and then to pull over to check for any damage before we continued on. We stopped under a flicking street light which produced very little light at all and turned the headlights off as normal to make sure that we didn't attract too much attention. District 8 was one of the safer districts in what was the old southwest of London but we were still not taking any chances. As we stopped and got out of the vehicle, Tom shouted from the back, "You could have fucking warned me about that as I wasn't strapped in you dicks", he was rubbing his head as he said it. I chuckled to myself and Nigel turned around and just laughed at him. I expected nothing less from him as in the nicest possible way, Nigel was mental.

It was my turn to be the first one out to scan the area for safety. I grabbed my assault rifle and body armour from the gun rack, attached a torch to the under rail of the gun and checked it a few times to make sure it was working properly. Since the waves had started, rolling blackouts were common and often lasted most of the night so a good touch was needed. I picked up a few clips of ammo and attached them to the body armour, loaded one into the rifle and cocked it. God, I loved this sound. I flipped the safety off, unlocked the armoured door and took a deep breath preparing to exit the safety of the Beast. I could hear Nigel and Tom suiting up, too. Tom would be covering the rear and I would be on point while Nigel assessed for any damage to our mobile home. Because we had been together for a decent period of time, we had formulated plans for this sort of situation. Whoever was driving checked for any damage while the other two of his scanned and surveyed the area and covered the one looking the Beast over.

I opened the door and stepped onto the pavement and I instantly went down onto one knee. I lifted the scope to my eye and scanned the area in front of me. I could see a shop front with smashed windows up ahead. To the left, I could see general debris and rubble and to my right, there was a pile of bricks which looked like an old barricade. I moved to the front of the vehicle and scanned the area.

There were a few cars that were stripped leaving mainly the shell. I stopped and listened for a moment. I could hear distant gun fire to the west but there was nothing that seemed close. So, I called for Tom to get out and heard the door slam shut followed by his boots on the ground. Tom quickly gave an all clear to Nigel who then jumped out and started inspecting his beloved Beast. Nigel inspected the damage and luckily, there was nothing too bad. He was just removing some debris from the windshield when a whoosh went past my head and struck the rubble beside me. More noise followed when I realized that it was gunfire. Hot metal landed on my arm so I dove to the ground in behind a pile of bricks.

Rounds came flying in nonstop piercing metal and shattering glass all around us. Tom and Nigel both opened the doors on the side of the vehicle to offer some extra protection. I crawled back towards them to use the doors as protection as well while covered me firing round after round into the distance. Tom was using a Bullpup Multirole which had a 30-round magazine and was using single shot. We couldn't really determine where the rounds were coming from apart from somewhere near a building in front of us. We knew that we had to act quickly as the beast was taking a pounding.

We heard someone shout in the distance, "Keep firing! We need that truck!" Tom looked down and me on laid out on the ground and shouted, "Get into the cab, turn the lights on full beam and start the engine. On my cue, get ready to hit reverse and get us the hell out of here! "His eyes did not leave the iron sight of his gun and I didn't need to be asked twice. Nigel was now moving round the passenger side laying down covering fire with his M16 Rifle but he had a drum magazine on his with a 100 round capacity and he was not taking pot shot. He was putting as many rounds as possible towards the shooters aiming at us. I picked myself up off the ground, slung my rifle over my shoulder and unholstered my sidearm. I kept it level with my eyes in case I needed it and dove into the driver's side with bullets smashing into the windshield but luckily, none passing through. I flicked the light switch to high beam and the street lit up and then started the engine. We had installed extra lights on the top of the Beast which came in handy now as looking into them was pretty similar to steering into the sun. The relentless noise stopped for a split second.

"GO, GO, GO", Tom said as he and Nigel dove in the front of the cab with me. I put the truck in reverse and floored the accelerator. The tires screeched as we started moving backwards. Gun fire picked up again with rounds hitting the windshield. I rammed a car shell off of the road that was behind us and pulled sideways into a street before putting it into first and setting off. We decided to drive without stopping and head to a safe zone just on the edge of District 15. We would often stay there in between travelling around and had discovered a compound with high walls, a secure gate and security cameras. It used to be an old warehouse. The walls were made of concrete and the gate was solid. We were certain to keep it looking run down and unused so that nobody would think it was worth having a look in but inside it was kind of like home to us when not in the Beast.

It only took about an hour to drive to the compound. Thankfully, the remainder was uneventful journey. We didn't speak most of the way back. Once we arrived, Nigel jumped out and opened the gate as I parked the beast in the vehicle bay and we covered it up with sheeting. As it was still evening, Tom and Nigel went to their rooms while I stood watch. I was exhausted, too, but could hopefully sleep in the morning. We felt fairly safe here and had driven these streets for many waves now and never came under attack. I didn't like gunfire but it was necessary today to survive. Hearing the shots ringing out, brought back all sorts of feelings and memories. My mind went dark and my eyes glazed over and I saw Ross laying there in a pool of blood. I shivered at his image and tried to think of something less sad. I then remembered back to when all of this started and of Summer, who I think saved me. Maybe she didn't actually leave me to die. I wondered where she might be and how she is holding up. I managed a slight smile when I thought about her body. I hadn't seen or even touched another girl in over a year so I started to get a little too excited thinking about her and realized it was time to stop. Over thinking was not going to help. I can't live in the past and I can't predict the future. I am lucky to be alive so I really need to concentrate on survival now. I grabbed my assault rifle and held it close and for the rest of the night I stood monitoring the compound until the morning.

It was about 6:00 a.m. when Nigel came walking over to me. "Here you go, kid. Have a cuppa. You look like shit", he said in a reassuring and calm voice passing me my favourite mug. On the front of it was

Mr. Messy. This is what my mam used to call me so I always had a fondness for this character.
"Thanks", I said as I took a mouth full of tea and wandered off back to my room to catch some sleep. I managed a good six hours of sleep that morning but my dreams were vivid, terrifying and traumatic. Night terrors were becoming almost routine.

When I was finally ready to get up, I grabbed a quick wash and caught up with Nigel and Tom. Nigel was outside fixing the Beast. It had been riddled with bullet holes which he was filling and Tom was welding some new metal plates to cover some of the bigger holes. The windshield looked as if it was starting to shatter from the impact of the rounds it took. "So, it looks like we need a new windshield before we can head out again", I said to Nigel. I was very good pointing out the obvious but since I had little engineering skills, I wasn't much help. " Yeah, that's not going to take many more hits before it shatters. I know a place in District 12 that will do be able to sort this out. Remember when we took it there when Tom, over here, decided to drive into a lamppost!" Nigel jabbed Tom in the ribs as he said this and Tom responded, "It looks like it's time for another road trip". District 12 would take around 3 hours reach even though London had an eighth of the population that it used to. So, the long drive wasn't due to excessive traffic but rather the wreckage, blockades, army patrols and maniacs with guns. Tom and Nigel finished the repairs as best as they could. They had added a type of cage covering over the front windshield which we "borrowed" off of a police riot van that we found nearby. We suited up, packed a little more ammo than last time and grabbed some water and food for the journey as we wanted to be there before sundown and didn't plan on travelling again until the following morning.

We had been driving for nearly two hours and making slow progress when we entered the rough area of District 13. Nigel and Tom were playing eye spy in the front and I was sitting in one of the rear compartments reading a programming book I had found in the back of a car a few months ago. The book was pretty advanced but it had vastly improved my knowledge of coding. I had picked up Python, C++, Java and Perl and I hadn't been able to practice much but when we got back to the compound, I would often try and put what I had learned into some sort of practical use. After all, there was very little else to do these days. I had managed to salvage a laptop I found and had basically managed to program a few smaller programs on the boring overwatch shift. It was sometimes nice to be able to take my mind off of things and get my head stuck around something other than this new life thrust upon us all.

"Eye spy with my little eye something beginning with N", I heard Tom say. "Ummm, not sure", Nigel responded eventually after a long pause while racking his brains. "Is that burning I can smell?", I shouted. "Fuck off", Nigel snapped back and they both giggled. "NERDDDDDDDDD", in unison was thrown back at me. This was the usual response from them when I was reading. This time, a ball was thrown at me narrowly missing my head. I could tell this was going to be a long journey. We rounded a corner and I was jolted forward.

"What the fuck, Tom", I shouted rather angrily. "there's a roadblock up ahead", shouted Nigel, "and it's a big one by the looks of it. We are going to have to back track or get out and have a look."
To be honest, neither seemed like a safe option so I went to stand up to walk to the front of the cab and I heard what sounded like a revving engine but it wasn't ours. I turned around and looked out of a slit cut into the side compartment and saw headlights hurtling towards us. "TOOOOOOOOMMMMMMM FL......", I tried to shout but before I could finish my sentence, I heard a loud bang and was hurtled through the air. I lost track of how many times the Beast rolled in the air but the noise was horrific and came to rest upside down. My head hit against one of the bulkheads, my ears were ringing, my head was pounding and my vision was blurred. I tried shaking my head to clear how I felt. I could make out some shouting but couldn't quite pinpoint who or where. My vision was coming back slowly and I could see figures now in front of the cab. The side door was yanked opened and I watched as Tom and Nigel were dragged out by men. I wondered what to do. If I shouted, they may come after me. Maybe they didn't see me yet. But if I didn't do anything, they might find not me but I had to help my friends. I checked my holster and found that my pistol was still there. My rifle was in the storage area at the front so I could discount grabbing that but my sidearm would give me a good level of protection as it was a Glock 9mm. Even though I had practiced with it many times, thanks to Nigel, I had never had to use it. But I had a feeling this was about to come to an end. I unclipped the flap of my holster and cocked the pistol slowly and as quietly as possible and crawled as

far forward as I dared listening for any noise. I could now make out voices and what they were saying.

"So, we finally got you! Remember us from yesterday? We have been tracking you for some time now. Do you have anything valuable in the truck?", a man said. However, I couldn't see him properly due to the smoke coming from the Beast. I didn't hear Tom or Nigel respond but the man laughed and smashed his rifle into one of them as all I saw a body slump over as he did. This had to stop now. They mustn't know that I am here. I crawled backwards towards the rear doors which were slightly ajar from the impact and I stumbled out and onto the street below. The Beast had come to rest against a brick wall. The truck which rammed us was in the middle of the road and was some sort of home delivery truck. I moved around the side of the Beast with my Glock raised and the safety off. It was hard to make out in the low light and smoke haze but I could see what I was assuming was Nigel and Tom on the ground. One was on their knees with their hands behind their back and one was laying on the ground. There were two men armed with baseball bats. The third man was standing over Nigel's body and holding a shotgun to what my eyes now focused to be Tom's head. The man with the gun was shouting at Tom but he wasn't answering. So, he smashed him in the face with the butt of the shotgun and blood went flying from his mouth. Now both of my friends were on the ground unable to run away. The men were laughing as they watched them drop. I didn't know what to do So many thoughts entered my head. Should I fire a warning shot? Should I just run away? I had no idea and wished someone was here to guide me. I was so used to working as part of a team with these guys that now it was up to me and me only to do the right thing but I didn't know what that was. I knew that I couldn't abandon my friends. This man would surely kill them if I didn't do something. I came up with a plan. I decided that I would make my way behind their truck, come out from behind the man with the shotgun and with a gun to his head, try and resolve this with no blood shed. Hopefully, all of this would be over and we could go our separate ways.

I was snapped out of my thoughts by the man kicking Tom in the stomach. He screamed in pain and rolled over. That was it. This was not going to go peacefully and this man was going to pay. I knew I had to do this now and do it quickly. I ran from behind the Beast towards the back of their truck. Nigel spotted me and shook his head and gestured with his eyes to go away. Luckily, nobody else had saw me. I walked as quietly as I could from behind the man and around to the front and held my gun to the man's head that had hurt my friends. "Put the shotgun down and tell your friends to back the FUCK away NOW." Who just spoke that forcefully? Was that my voice? The man stood still for a second and then placed the shotgun on the ground. "Back away now lads", he said in a typical cockney accent. I took a step back to give Nigel some room to get up and tend to Tom. I cleared my throat and tried not to sound like I was scared shitless. "You will stay exactly as you are. We are going to leave in your truck. Don't try and follow us. Nigel, lift Tom up and bring him to the truck while I keep you covered", and he picked Tom up.

Just then as Nigel and Tom got up, a horrible realization dawned on me as I noticed something in my peripheral vision. There was a fourth man who had remained quiet and had been standing out of my view to the side of the beast with an assault rifle. I saw him when he lifted his rifle to aim it at Nigel. "DO NOT MOVE!", he shouted. "Now lower your fucking weapons and kick them over to me!" The man that had the shotgun laughed, "Ha! You missed him, didn't you? Now what you going to do, you scrawny twat?" That unfortunately was a valid point. What was I going to do? I was seriously now outgunned. But I did have the shotgun guy between myself and the one with the assault rifle and I still did have the pistol pointed at his head. But Tom and Nigel were completely out in the open.

"Don't you dare drop your gun", Nigel said. I could see him eyeing up the shotgun and it was just within his arm's reach. Adrenaline was now kicking in and fear was leaving my body but my arm was trembling and a tear ran down my face. I was terrified that one wrong move would end us all and I had no idea how to even begin to get out of this situation. "BOY, PUT THE GUN DOWN AND NOBODY WILL GET HURT! Now, I'll say it one last time, lower your handgun and kick it over to me." However, I knew that this meant put the gun down and we WILL hurt you. Before I knew what was happening, I watched Nigel lunge for the shotgun, rip it out of the man's hands and shoot the man with the assault rifle. At the exact same time, the man with the assault rifle fired back towards Nigel. I heard four rounds disburse and three of those hit Nigel directly in his chest with the fourth hitting Tom in his stomach. Three men lay slumped over on the ground and two of them were the last of my friends. I saw blood burst out of the wound in Tom's stomach. Just then, Mr. Shotgun lunged for the shotgun on the ground. I couldn't let him get it and I lifted my Glock, squeezed its trigger and one round left my chamber directly into the back of his head. I could see skull fragments shatter as his blood sprayed all over Nigel's lifeless body. And with that, Mr. Shotgun slumped to the ground. I glanced sideways and the two men with baseball bats charged towards me. I was shaking but had to compose myself so I fired another round into the guy to my left striking him in the chest and quickly turned to the guy to my right and fired two rounds into him. One hit him in the shoulder and the other in the neck. Both went down to the ground and neither were never getting up again. I dropped my pistol and just stood there for a few seconds. Reality started to return as my adrenaline subsided. What the fuck had just happened? How did playing eye spy one-minute lead to this? I checked on Nigel. He had no pulse. I looked over to Tom who was bleeding heavily and I cradled him in my arms. "Tom, it's going to be ok. I'm going to get the first aid kit from the Beast and I'll be right back", he looked into my eyes. "No mate, don't bother. It's not worth it, just, just, just...." His eyes closed and his head rolled to the side. "FUCKKKKKKKKKKKKKKKKKK!!", I shouted out loud and I held Tom as close as possible and rocked him back and forth. "Don't die man. Please don't die. You are the last person I have left", there was no answer. His body was limp. Blood was trickling out of his mouth and I sat there for a moment weeping. But I then heard a groan coming from beside the truck. It was the man who shot Tom and

Nigel. I felt rage building up inside of me that I had never before. I got up, picked up my pistol and walked towards him. He looked at me and whispered, “Help me.” My reply? “Fuck you” and I raised my pistol and unloaded the clip into him. I kept squeezing the trigger until the magazine was empty. I ejected that magazine and loaded another one. Every single round went into that man but he deserved it. I walked back over to Nigel and Tom feeling numb. The rage that I felt just now burned away any sadness and emotion. I was not crying or angry. I just stood and stared at their lifeless corpses with a renewed sense of loneliness. I decided at this point that I was done losing people and done with life in the districts. I was going to head to District Z on my own and do something. Anything. I didn't know what but that was my plan. I got all the useful supplies out of the wreckage of the Beast then I placed the bodies of Nigel and Tom inside and poured petrol over them. I held a moment's silence and said a prayer for them as I watched over them one last time. I decided that this was the best way for them to go as I was not going to let them be dug up by some scavenger or even worse, an alien. I managed to get the other truck started and jumped in. As I started to pass the remains of what was the Beast, I stopped for a moment, remembered my friends then tossed in a flare. I could feel the heat immediately as the fire intensified with the added fuel and I drove off into the darkness to face an even more uncertain future.

Chapter X - Mr. Boney McBoneFace

I had to ditch the truck just outside of District Z due to the amount of army patrols and security in the area. One view of the truck and I wouldn't like to think what would happen to me. I packed as much as I could carry including supplies, weapons and ammo and dumped the truck in a carpark about 500 meters from the border. Luckily at this point, it was pretty dark and streets were deserted this close to the crash site.

District Z was by no means super secure like the DMZ or the old M25. There were FOBs, patrols and CCTV but the gaps in the security were numerous because of how regimented the military. Often soldiers would get bored after spending months and months in the same area and they'd wander off. I had been to this area a few times just more out of interest than anything else and I knew I could get in with relative ease once I checked the lay of the land. I walked 500 meters to the edge of the zone where I could see the first signs of it being a no-go district. Signs instructing "Military only", "DO NOT CROSS", "CCTV operates in this area". Everything that you would expect to see in a zone that I probably should not be heading into. But I had my reasons to go there. It should be relatively safe as long as I didn't get caught. I could always raid supply depots for food.

This area is where this nightmare all started for me. By now, I was seeing daylight so I decided to not risk crossing open land at this time. Next to where I was standing was an office building that looked to be about twenty stories high. Everything looked pretty intact which I wasn't used to seeing in the other districts. The building was glass fronted and had a wooden panel with a padlock covering the front entrance. I searched around the grounds and picked up a brick and decided the fastest way inside was to smash the lock off. It worked. I made my way inside being careful not to make too much noise. Once inside, to my amazement, the building was in fair shape apart from some smashed windows which I am guessing was from the blast. It didn't appear as if anyone had been in here for a while. The floor was dusty and there wasn't any working electricity. But here were no visible signs of graffiti, looting or any other indication that it was occupied. I looked behind the reception desk and found a chest of drawers and dragged them over to block the now open door. Then I made a trip upstairs. I couldn't be certain that no one was upstairs so I unholstered my Glock, cocked it and flicked the safety off just in case. I continued to move up the building floor by floor checking every area but this building had been left in the exact same condition as the day the previous occupants left, I'm guessing. I found paperwork, packed lunch boxes and I made the horrible mistake of opening a fridge that hadn't been used for a long time with no power. I finally made it to the top floor. I had climbed 18 floors and it took a while to check every area. I noticed a ladder going up to the roof and I decided before I tried to get some sleep, that I was going to head up there and see what I could. It should give me a great view across the area. I needed to make sure that I could pinpoint where I was going and would be able to check for patrols. I stashed my bag of supplies in a small cupboard beside the ladder. Keeping my trusty sidearm attached, I climbed the ladder and opened the hatch on the roof. As I did, a pigeon flew in front of me nearly giving me a heart attack.

I lifted myself up onto the roof, took my binoculars from around my neck and looked out as far as I could see. There it was. I could see it. District Y. And what I believe to be District X as well. I finally had my first glance of what had hit London. The oval shaped objects were standing about ten stories tall with a metallic coating on them. I could only see parts of them as they were covered in sheeting and scaffolding. I could make out military vehicles and some sort of base beside each one. It looked as if buildings had been flattered around them. I'm guessing from impact or for greater visibility to keep an eye on them. It was an awe inspiring yet terrifying site. I just stood there looking for who knows how long remembering what had happened just a few hours ago and within the last year. None of the loss I've experienced would've happened if it hadn't been for whatever these things were. I had been totally lost in my thoughts when I heard a noise that I couldn't decipher. But then it came into focus and shit! It was a Black Hawk helicopter and was maybe 600 meters away heading straight for me. I quickly assessed my options. The hatch was on the other side of the roof and I wasn't sure that I could make it in time. If the pilot noticed anything moving, like me, they may shoot at me. 500 meters. Fuck, I need to move and quickly. I noticed a pile of rags beside me and I decided this was my best option. I dove towards them and quickly threw them all over my body but as a few rags wouldn't move, I then realized that they were attached to a skeleton. Oh my God. I was lying next to a dead person's bones and it was their clothing that I was covering myself with. I could hear the helicopter getting closer but it flew over a nearby building only a few meters away missing the one that I was hiding on but the downdraft blew the rags off of me. I then saw the poor person's bones whose clothes I had ripped off of them. I just laid there for a few minutes afraid to move and waited for everything to go quiet again. Once I couldn't hear anything, not even a peep, I decided to sit up and look around. I noticed the skull lying beside me. It had a bullet hole right through it. As I continued to comb down the roof with my eyes, I saw a pistol. I couldn't help but wonder if he took his own life or did someone else do it for him. A backpack lay nearby the pistol so I went over to view its contents. It contained some canned food, ammo and a thick fleece which I thought might come in handy tonight. This poor man, at least I think it was, didn't realize it but in his death, he was helping me by providing me with an extra gun and a warm blanket.

Morning came and I was awakened by a bird singing. I just lay there on the dusty floor of an empty office building and listened to its song for a while. In this crazy world, it wasn't very often that we could just listen to something so simple and peaceful. I had learned a little about a practice called 'mindfulness' which is thinking of the present and taking in what's around you, the sights, sounds and smells of the world. That was all fine and good before any of this happened. Now, if you weren't on your toes and thinking ahead, you were as good as dead. This reality ruined the peaceful moment that I was having so I got up and headed down a corridor. I found what appeared to be the executive bathroom. There were gold plated taps, the sinks were designer looking and there was even a shower. I hadn't had a shower in a while. My clothes were covered in dried blood and muck as was I and I smelled badly. I found a few lockers in the corner and smashed the locks off of them. Inside were a few items of clothing which would do just fine. They looked a bit big but they surprisingly smelled clean and fresh or it maybe it was just that I smelled so much worse at the moment. I turned on the shower and was surprised that it still worked given that there was no electricity in the building. Maybe this is what was left in the reserve tank so I better make it quick before it ran out. It most likely would not be warm in any way. I stepped into the shower after finding some shower gel in one of the lockers. The pipes banged for a second and the water started out of the showerhead in short bursts before settling on a small stream. Yes, it was indeed cold but running water had become a luxury in London as it was scarce with only the rich being able to afford such things. I think about twenty waves had passed since I last had a shower. It was freezing but it was bliss.

I slipped into some fresh clothes, sprayed some deodorant on that I had found and headed down to the boardroom to plan my next move. I searched around the offices for a while looking for a local map. I was able to find one on the wall of some sort of sales office. I ripped it down, grabbed some highlighters and headed back to the boardroom. I had no idea why I wanted to head into this dangerous zone and I knew that there was a high probability that I may die. I laid the map out on the boardroom table and located the area where the swimming pool was. It looked to be roughly under a kilometre away from where I was. I marked several routes to cover most situations that could possibly arise. In this zone, I may not get eaten by wild wolves or killed by insane folk or scavengers but I had to keep an eye out for military snipers, infrared cameras and routine patrols. I decided on trying to make it back to the swimming pool area as that's where I was on the happiest day of my life between my interview with GREYSOFT and meeting Summer. And this was before my best friends had been killed. Maybe if I backtracked, I'd somehow strangely feel closer to that day and not like my entire world had been ripped away from me.

I decided to travel by day as patrols didn't frequent this area much it seemed. Their attention seemed fixed more on Districts X and Y. Plus, I had no advanced equipment so night time travel would be more than tough.

Since I had about fifteen hours before I planned to set off, I ransacked the place. I was a fan of survival games back before all of this. "7 Days to Die", "Day Z" and "Playerunknown's Battlegrounds". All of these games taught that scavenging was surviving. I searched until evening while there was still daylight and then at night, I gathered all my finds together. By my count, I had enough food now to last about two weeks if I rationed properly, I had plenty of bottled water, I had my assault rifle with two mags of ammunition and three spare rounds so sixty-five in total, a pistol with three mags, a knife, a sleeping bag and a few other bits and bobs I had found that may come in handy like a jacket and some extra socks. And of course, the clothes on my back, my body armour and some tactical gloves. I looked out of the window facing east across London and noticed the sun was rising. What a beautiful sight! I hadn't watched a sunrise in a long time so I decided to head to the roof and watch it from there. I grabbed my sleeping bag and climbed up the ladder.

I tucked my sleeping bag under my head to use as a pillow and lay beside the skeleton's remains which I decided in this lovely tranquil moment to name "Mr. Boney McBoneface" and watched the sunrise. I must've laid there for nearly an hour. With my eyes closed, I could almost hear the hustle and bustle of what London used to be like and the faint voice of a weatherman saying "Today, London will be glorious with wall to wall sunshine so have a good day out their people of London." I was snapped out of my daydream when I heard distant gunshots and a helicopter firing off in the distance. I said my goodbyes to Mr. Boney McBoneface, grabbed my stuff and headed off on my journey to the swimming pool.

Chapter XI - Changing Room

It took about an hour to reach District X and surprisingly, nothing went horribly wrong. I was still on the outskirts of the centre of the District but I found a second hand shop that had a few books in it so I poked around and found a few that I'd not read before. "Harry Potter and the Cursed Child" 1 & 2, "The Serpent King", "Boy X" by Dan Smith and most ironically "Reasons to Stay Alive" by Matt Haig. I tucked them away in my backpack and as I did, I could hear both Tom and Nigel yelling "NERRRRRRD". Man, I missed them. I nearly stepped on a Lego set hiding under some debris. I picked it up and brushed the dirt and rubble off of it. Number #70916 Lego Movie Batwing. Since I was alone now, I needed activities to keep my mind active so I'd not end up like Tom Hanks in "Castaway" talking to volleyball. But just in case, I tucked a nearly flattened volleyball under my arm to cover all of my bases.

The one thing that was noticeable as I got closer to the swimming pool was the destruction. The roads had been mainly cleared by the army so the pavement was piled high with bricks, cars and bits of buildings, office furniture and all sorts of other debris. What hit me the most were the personal items. Bags, chairs, children's toys. I know death had become an everyday occurrence now but to think that on this very spot, people were once alive going about their lives and now they were gone. I wondered how many had died and how many had escaped. This reflection on life stirred emotions that I locked away since rage filled me. I started to think of how many people like me had lost loved ones and family. My mind started racing, sadness washed over me and in the middle of a deserted street, all alone, surrounded by damaged buildings, I put my head in my hands and sobbed. My mind was cloudy and dark and this seemed like the only way that I could clear it. My chest felt tight, my heart rate increased. I'm not sure how long I stood there but it felt like years passed. My God, did that feel good but I pulled myself together. I had always heard that sometimes it's best just to let it all out and have a good cry. I never believed it before now I did now. I felt really fresh and clear and I ran the rest of the way to the swimming pool.

It was just as I remembered it minus the ball of fire and a hot girl beside me but apart from that, not too much seemed to have changed. My plan was to secure the building as best I could. I did think maybe "Home Alone" style with toy cars on the floor or maybe something a little more robust. I needed to find somewhere to set up a small camp if I wanted a safe escape route. I walked towards the main entrance, unslung my rifle off of my back and brought it up so the stock rested against my shoulder. I laid down my backpack in the entrance way so I'd not lose it. I flicked on the torch under the barrel attachment of the AR-15 and made sure my body armour was tight. From the many waves that brought about scavenging, I had done this many times but not without backup. To the left of the entrance was a clearing sticker indicating that no bodies remained. These were massive red stickers that could be seen on most of the buildings around here. The first area that I walked into was the foyer. The electric barriers were still there and the ticket booth was somewhat there; however, most of the glass had being blown out from the explosion when the “asteroid” hit. I scanned left and right and saw nothing. I stood still for a moment and listened carefully. Again, nothing. There was a thick dusting of debris on the floor that would’ve indicated if anyone had been here. I made a mental note to be sure to cover my own tracks. I moved forward slowly towards the ticket booth and continued toward the pool area scanning all around me as I did. The changing rooms were to the left as I remembered. I decided to turn off my torch as it was now pretty bright with the missing roof. I got closer to the swimming pool expecting to see it full of water but apart from a few puddles, it was empty. Debris was littered about everywhere and a crack in the pool exposed a small channel of water which is where I guessed the water had gone. I scanned the changing rooms and found no movement or signs of life. It didn’t look like anyone had been here since I was last here. I lowered my rifle, slung it over my shoulder keeping the safety off and drew my pistol from my holster. I went back to the entrance to grab my stuff and was careful to follow my footsteps so they were easier to cover. I grabbed my backpack and as I did, I swept with my hand the remaining debris over my footprints which worked remarkably well.

I walked around the swimming pool and found a store room at the back with a lock still in place but managed to find the keys on the floor nearby. I set up my sleeping bag and put my stuff on the racks, locked the door and grabbed some shut eye. Securing this place and setting up traps could wait until evening. For now, I was safe.

I had no idea what time it was when I woke but the sun was starting to get low in the sky and I needed to get to work. I decided that the swimming pool was way too exposed to the elements considering it had a gaping hole in one side. The store room was secure but way too small. I decided not to touch the foyer as the amount of debris and dust left undisturbed would give people the impression it was abandoned and they'd not come in. So, this left the changing rooms. There were only two doors in and one I was going to barricade. Inside there was a lot of space. I could store my supplies, assemble a few different firing positions plus there were toilets, showers, mirrors. Really all I needed. The one downside was no obvious escape route. But I decided to tackle that issue in a bit.

I decided to go a bit "Home Alone" and found some string some empty cans. I wanted to set up a few early warning noise devices in case anyone decided to try and enter. I managed to manoeuvre a few lockers in front of one of the doors and followed those up with some benches and chairs. I was working up a sweat. Thankfully, I had showers close by. I then began crafting my basic noise devices with a thin piece of wire attached to can filled with some debris that would rattle if anyone tripped over it. I also planned to make a bigger one for the front entrance. I then scattered some broken glass in key areas so that if anyone did come in, I would hopefully hear it crack under their feet. After setting up all of my traps, I constructed a bit of a living area which took the rest of the night. I set up to the back of the changing room and moved a set of lockers around to form a type of square around me with the lockers facing inwards so they could be used for storage. I then set up a bench and some swim mats on the floor for a bit of a softer flooring and left one side with a gap of about 3ft wide away from the open door facing the showers so if anyone came in, they wouldn't see me. I had found part of the cover for the swimming pool and put that over the top and tried my best to tie it down. I selected a few lockers and made a hole in the back with my knife just big enough for my rifle muzzle. I figured in an emergency, I could fire through them or use them as a peep hole or both. I then selected a few lockers for supplies near the makeshift door for a quick getaway. I reached into my bag and pulled the map out. I stuck this on one side of the lockers so that I could keep an eye on places I wanted to raid and check off places I had been. I found a plank of wood which I stored my Lego set and new books on and used the larger locker for my guns and body armour. Not bad for a night's work. By the end, it looked pretty impressive. A little homey, too, I thought.

The sun was rising as I could see it coming through the open door. I needed to get some cover for the door, too, to try and keep the heat in. But I was too tired right now and unrolled my sleeping bag and went to sleep. It was one of the best night's sleep that I've had in a long time. My dreams were all happy. No night terrors. I dreamt of Summer, my friends and my family. I didn't realize that I was dreaming until I was stirring and woken up rudely by a large drop of water. I had missed a hole in my temporary roof. This was my que to get up and wonder about. I explored a little more today around the ticket office and found another storage area with lots of food like pasta and some dried soups. Much to my delight, I found a rowing machine. I was mainly fit from running around carrying heavy backpacks but this was an ideal way to keep fit. I dragged it into what I deemed "Matthew's Fortress of Solitude". Yes, I named it and yes, I made a sign with some spray paint I found. I think calling it a fortress was slightly overselling it but my luck was changing. I also found a gas grill outback with a few gas bottles. Hot food sounded awesome right now; however, where I would find anything useful was another matter. But I could use the gas to boil water which would come in handy. I set this up in one of the shower areas as a bit of a cooking zone. I kept one shower for washing, one for cooking and the final set of showers would be my way out of here if needed. I hoped under the shower that the drainage for this place would go into the same area towards the pool then out into the sewers somewhere. I already noted the channel the rain water was escaping through. Besides, I had seen many films like the "Rock" with Nicholas Cage. Showers were always hollow underneath. My plan for escape included digging a hole under the shower floor to expose the drainage and then jump into it if I needed to quickly escape. I had no practical engineering experience or knowledge. I was pretty terrible with tools but this was just bashing a big hole into the ground and how hard could that be! But first, I needed something like a pickaxe to get through the tiles and then maybe a shovel or sledgehammer to clear the rest. This was going to be the hard part. I needed some sort of builder's merchants or hardware store to find these sorts of items and I didn't remember seeing one. But the second issue posed is the NOISE. Someone would definitely hear that! After all, the streets are very quiet but snipers could be wandering around. Maybe I was overthinking things as I did have a habit of that. Always looking for the most complex way to do things. I went over to the shower area to pull the drain up from my "escape hatch". I had to use some twisted metal that I found and using my weight as a countermeasure, I managed to lift it up. Under the drain was a pipe. I grabbed my gun and shined the light down below and sure enough, it seemed to lead into a bigger pipe. I picked up a stone and dropped it. 1 Mississippi, 2 Mississippi, 3 Miss.... *plop* I heard the sound. Perfect. Not too far. Unfortunately, the entrance down wasn't big enough for me to fit through so I decided to rethink this one and I changed my escape plan slightly to a riskier one. I'd make a small gap in the lockers in front of the blocked door just big enough for me to squeeze through if needed. It wasn't the best plan but it's all I had for now until I could find the necessary tools to rip up the shower floor. I now had a risky escape plan, a makeshift kitchen, a home gym and a wash area. I double checked my supplies managed to collect about a month of food. Life didn't seem to be going too badly in my little fortress of solitude.

It took a total of 4 waves for me to finally break through the pipe under the shower for my escape route. I had to do it quietly and time it with helicopters flying by, tanks rolling past or sirens in the distance. I searched high and low in the local area for tools and all I could find was a very small pick axe. Either side of the pipe was pure concrete and it took a lot of effort to make the hole. When I eventually broke the main pipe, I climbed along the pipeline and directly under the swimming pool and out into the sewers just below. I decided I didn't really want to end up in the sewers. YUCK! So I managed to build what I called the "London Deep Poo Dam" to separate the sewer from the water waste pipe I didn't want any risk of it coming getting anywhere near the waste pipe and I made a makeshift ladder out of rope and a few scraps of wood up to a manhole cover above. It came out just behind the swimming pool and there was my escape route. I positioned the remaining lockers to provide cover in case I needed it to what I referred to as "Escape Hatch One" and blocked the other entrance back up.

I decided to celebrate as that very day on one of my scavenging runs, I found some canned chicken, three bottles of Strongbow cider and some chocolate pudding. I drank merrily, ate well and chilled the hell out now that my little area was safe and mainly secure. It wasn't very often in today's world that I got the chance to do this so I took it while I could. But I forgot one vital thing, cider made me sleep too soundly and I never heard what was coming.

Chapter XII - Sal

I was awakened by a loud squealing noise. Instinctively before opening my eyes, I reached for my gun but my hand felt numb. I couldn't feel it. I gave myself a little pep talk, "Come on, Matthew, open your eyes. You need to see what's happened."

I knew I had fallen asleep. Was this it? Had I been taken? I slowly opened my eyes and discovered that I was surrounded by a light blue haze. I reached out with my other hand to touch it and I could feel it but I could not reach though it. It was like some sort of barrier or forcefield. I started to look round through the haze. I could see that I was still in my fortress of solitude but apart from my head and my left arm I couldn't move. It felt like something was holding me down; however, I noticed outside the bubble that things seemed a little odd. The water dripping from the ceiling was just sort of hanging there suspended. I could see dust particles in the air that were not moving. It was like time had stopped.

I noticed a flash of light just behind the lockers but was unable to see what it was. This was it. I lay back and accepted my fate. I had lasted maybe a thousand waves, in old money that was over three years, and now because of some celebrating, I was done in. That was the end of Matthew. I then saw it for the first time. The figure was about 7' and slender in appearance. It didn't seem to have a distinct outline and was emitting a purple haze around itself. There were no noticeable features. No face. No clothes. No hair. Just pure blackness which made it stand out against the dimly lit background. Whatever it was, drew closer and I noticed what I assumed were two eyes but not in the human sense. They were like two glowing orbs with an almost hypnotical beauty within like galaxies swirling about in them. The figure was now merely 4 feet away and yet still I couldn't make anything out apart from those eyes. I couldn't help but look into them. They were mesmerizing. It was now standing at the edge of the barrier and looking right at me. My skin was chilled, goose bumps covered every inch of my body as the figure moved an outstretched arm lifted my rifle off of the ground. The clip fell out and the safety flicked then the rifle was gently lowered back to the ground. Then this thing, this creature, raised its other arm and I was unable to move at all. I could only look straight up like I was trapped in place. I tried to scream but couldn't. No noise came out of my mouth at all. I've suffered from sleep paralysis before and this felt like exactly that. Maybe I was just dreaming all of this. The barrier then came down and the figure walked towards me and touched my head. I could feel something going into my ear that felt metallic and cold. I tried to resist and move but I couldn't. The figure then stepped back and the barrier enveloped around me again. I was then able to fully move. Instantly, I jumped up and clung to the back of the barrier.

"Who the fuck are you? What do you want? Let me out now!" There was no answer. "Look, whatever you are, my name is Matthew. I am alone in here. Could you please let me go? I don't want to be taken." My annoyance was followed by sobbing as a mixture of emotions washed over me from sadness to fear but almost a sense of relief that I wasn't fighting anymore. Still no answer. "Will you just get it over and done with? I accept my fate." I was definitely flying through the seven stages of grief here. Still no answer. This was getting annoying now so I banged on the barrier and swore some more. I am not sure why I suddenly decided to act like a caged monkey but I decided all else had failed. I heard a faint crackle in my ear then a voice. I was unable to make it out at first as it took a few minutes to adjust. It sounded human but slow and controlled in how it spoke. I couldn't make out a word it was saying as it was too quiet. The figure seemed to move its arm towards its head and then suddenly I heard everything clearly.

"Will you stop acting like a primate and sit-down Matthew? We need to talk and I can't do this with you running around and shouting", it said. I sat there speechless. This thing was speaking. It continued "Now listen up, Matthew, we have much to cover. Let me introduce myself, my Earth name is Umbra Tenebrarum Consiliarius. Now I don't expect you know what that means but it stands for Dark Shadow Advisor. My sole purpose of this mission to the planet you call Earth is to act as what would you would call a humanitarian or overseer. My role here is to engage, talk, help and interact with the humans, learn the culture and help with the transplantation of humans from here to my home planet in a way to cause the least impact to your species. The planet that I am from is designated as Planetoid 52678-90 X by your home government. Do you have any questions so far?"
Again, I sat in silence for a few moments and all I could manage in my first proper exchange with an alien was, "What the Fuck?" I was

never cut out for first contact. The voice continued, "So you might be wondering why you haven't been transported to our vessel yet? And could we keep bad language to a minimum please. You humans seem to use it a lot!"
A few seconds past while I composed myself. "Well, the thought had crossed my mind, Umbro Tenebra Councillor" Meh, close enough. The figure sighed, "No, that isn't close enough." "You can read my thoughts?" "Yes, Matthew I can, and your emotions, too. By the way, It's Umbra Tenebrarum Consiliarius just to point that out. The device I inserted in your ear allows us to understand each other as we communicate. But I can also read your thoughts, too, so maybe stop thinking I sound like a bit of an asshole for an alien, too." I walked towards him and I tried to think of anything but what I wanted to think about. "Look, this is a bit much for me to take in. I have so many questions to ask and you caused the deaths of everyone I fucking love and care about AND almost killed me in the fucking process. I do have some more pressing questions but I am sure you already know what I am going to ask. First off, is there anything easier that I can call you?" He responded, "Well, as I am here to hopefully save humanity so you can call me Salvator."
"Salvator", I responded.
"It means Saviour in Latin. Don't you think it has a nice ring to it?" his voice in my ear was pretty sarcastic. "I'll tell you what, I'll call you Sal. How does that sound?" I decided it was time to throw an attitude back at him. Sal sighed, "If you must, can I continue now? We don't have much time."
"Be my guest, I'm not exactly going anywhere", and I sat on the bench to relax. "I know your anger is well placed but that will

hopefully pass in time so this is what you want to know." He passed me a device that kind of looked like a transparent iPhone. "This has a signal blocker in built which will hide your location. I am here unofficially and I have put myself in grave danger just to be here. This device will allow us to communicate easier on the move. It also has a sub mind of me in built into t for when I am not around. It can carry out a range of functions but if you think I'm an asshole then you may be in for a bit of a shock. Secondly, and this may annoy you a little, getting you to this location was no accident. I have been I guiding you to this location as our sensors have a blind spot in this certain area so they will be unable to track you." I interrupted Sal, "Hang on, you guided me? I'm confused. Why me? Why would you do this? This isn't the first time you've talked to me, is it?" Sal obviously knew what I was about to say before I even said. "Look, that would take too long to explain and I don't have the time. I need to get back to the ship. All I need you to do is stay alive, stay calm and I will be back in twenty-three of your earth hours" and with that, Sal floated off towards the back of the lockers. The bright light and the forcefield were gone.

I just lay there for a while taking it all in. I thought back over the past and it started to make sense a little. Certain decisions I made, how had I made it here without being seen or attacked. Had Sal played a part in this? There were so many questions that I had and I knew I would need to wait to get the answers. I scratched the inside of my ear and felt the metal device. It was half embedded in my ear and when I tried to pull it out, it wouldn't budge. I did contemplate trying to cut it out as I did not want this alien to know what I was thinking. I wondered if he could understand me now. I hoped not; otherwise, he would know the dark places my mind went, my darkest secrets, my greatest fears. This was something I didn't need him or want him to know. I made a mental note to talk about boundaries when he came back. After what seemed like a few hours, I finally got up and moved. It was now daylight and I checked the traps, carried out a detailed sweep of the area and made some breakfast. For the rest of the day, I mainly mentally prepared myself for the night ahead.

Darkness set in and I lay on my makeshift bed. Sal had told me that I couldn't be "relocated" so then I could sleep whenever I wanted to which felt like an amazing relief. Of course, if he was lying, I was basically screwed. I wasn't sure how I was going to sleep with this much anxiety and the fact that I hadn't slept during the night for a very long time.

I felt like I had just dozed off when I was awakened by a loud noise followed by a blinding white flash. Out from the shadows stepped Sal. The earpiece buzzed again. "Hey, Matthew, how are you today? I know you will have more questions and I will try to answer them but I don't have much time so choose them wisely." I was feeling more calm this time and no barrier had appeared and I wasn't paralysed so this visit was already starting off much better. "I'm kind of torn on my first question as I need to know why the HELL you, as you put it, guided me here? And why did you come to Earth at all and cause all of this death, destruction and pain? Feel free to answer either one first." I sat with my arms folded looking the other way like a child pouting. The initial surprise had been replaced with a real hatred of this thing. Whatever Sal was. I could sense a bit of sadness in the voice coming though this time. "Look, the loss of life was supposed to be minimised; however, due to the fact that Earth has six billion inhabitants, the loss of leaders was decided within acceptable limits." "Acceptable fucking limits", I shouted back, "By WHO?!" Sal continued ignoring my outburst, "I will keep it simple for you. Basically, I come from a planet far away. We were not very different from you in some ways. We, too, are contained in a body and over many millennia, we evolved to this form. But there were still some constraints that we couldn't overcome and large numbers of us were killed in the process. We suffered almost 90% loss in our population over one thousand Earth years. Evolution, it seemed, didn't work too well for our species and due to our now advanced nature, we lost the ability to repopulate and cloning techniques all but failed. The only way our species could survive is to repopulate our planet from native populations of other planets. We usually try negations beforehand but your Earth government was unwilling to negotiate with us. We assumed this was due your planet's lack of overall leadership, fighting amongst yourselves and world tension. For our survival, we had to arrive and in force. We only take a maximum of ten percent of any given population. They work our land, factories and help fight in our wars, as well as act as segregates for recreations of us which are used for keeping what's left of our population alive. The native population left on the planet become what is known as a client species to ours and we will offer protection from other alien factions, advanced medical supplies, technologies and weapons as compensation as well as uniting the planet and acting as mediators for governments." I looked at Sal and sighed, "Gee, thanks. Hey, we killed loads of you, caused billions in damages, stole a few millions of your citizens but here have a laser gun", I lay back down and just rolled over into the foetal position and cuddled into my blanket. I couldn't believe what I just heard.

"Yes, your government knew about us. They were also given enough time to negotiate. Did you not wonder how come there was such a quick military response to us landing?" He continued, "But they declined our offer and this is why we are here. Our council decided to go ahead without your civilization agreeing to our repopulation. Out of the 128 client species we have, you are the only planet who put life of the native population above the compensation that we were offering. This is when things changed on board our ship. I and two others on the council voted against this action and the repopulation; however, we were overruled. Matthew, I chose you to help me and to bring an end to the repopulation of this planet. I can't stand by anymore and let this happen. Usually we target less civilised and less evolved species but humans surprised me and I became fond of your kind. I was interrogating a human male you know as "Jon" and added you to a list of potential humans that could help me. I can't do it on my own as the council would notice that I was gone. I needed someone with survival skills and a high technical ability plus someone who could be guided to where I needed them to be and as you had lost everything, you became the perfect human. I have been tracking you and waiting for you to come back to a place where I could

communicate with you." I turned around to face Sal, "WAIT!! JON? Jon. Jon? You spoke to him?"
"Yes, I spoke to him before his relocation but he was the that final push I needed to do something about the mistreatment of humans in this way." I sighed heavily, "Just......You know what? FUCK YOU AND YOUR ALIEN FRIENDS!", I screamed as a tear ran down my eye. "No, you couldn't punch me, Matthew, you are too short and too slow. It actually hurts how behind your species is sometimes. So dumb! When you are not killing each other, you are insulting and fighting each other. No better than a cage full of primates. This will blow your tiny little mind but this isn't the first time we visited your planet. Remember learning about how dinosaurs were wiped out? Well, it wasn't a meteor. It was us. Our technology was a little less advanced then and we were new to space travel. Boy, A LOT changed in 65 million years, so yeah, our bad! However, we helped humanity to thrive and we set a timer for 65 million years and here we are! It was my job to research, watch and learn your culture to help with the relocation. So, to find that you still don't know how the dinosaurs were killed off amazes me. We actually have a small population on our planet and that T-REX is almost as grumpy as you." I turned back around, "You have dinosaurs on your home world? I have to be making this up now. I've finally gone insane and I'm in an insane asylum somewhere." Sal moved towards me, "Look, Matthew, there is still more that you need to know but my time is up again. I will explain more tomorrow. Don't worry, you're not insane. YET." He emphasised "yet". "Don't worry, this is all too real but I understand it must be hard to fathom with your teeny brain. I

will see you tomorrow" and with that he walked around the corner and vanished.

Why is he SUCH an ASSHOLE! Why, out of all of the aliens was this one offering to help humanity. But I thought that behind his seemingly arrogant ways, if he could help us stupid humans out then some help is better than nothing. Over the next few nights, I started sleeping consistently again now that Sal had promised me, he had removed me from the system of selected targets and I wouldn't be taken. He informed me that in total 2 MILLION people had been relocated from within a 20-mile radius of what he called it the holding vessel. They estimated that within 3 months, they would then move out and start taking people from Northern Europe and the rest of the UK. Testing had been done in these areas to track people and 1,000 people from these areas had been relocated in preparation. He informed me that usually, a client species is "willing "to give up 10% of its population and that they didn't have to rely on the technology to do the work. This is why it was so concentrated within a 20-mile radius while they refined their system and were sent new parts from their home planet to increase the ability and scale of the repopulation system. He tried to explain how it worked but of course, said I was too stupid to understand even in "IDIOT" terms. He said that everyone on earth was marked. Scouts would mark a certain amount of people and would wait until that person closed their eyes at night. A certain brain wave activity indicating REM sleep would initiate the transporter vessel to transport them. They would then be held, cleaned and medically assessed as to what task they would be carrying out. When I tried to elaborate on this, he changed the subject very quickly which made me worry. No matter how many times I pressed him on the issue, he would just move on or tell me it would be better if I didn't know. The marks would then be moved to the mothership in orbit and spend 3 months travelling back towards Sal's home planet. Unfortunately, because humanity had declined to do this voluntarily, they would be taking about 30-40% of the population of Earth and no technology would be given in return. However, humans would become a client species and fall under the protection of the great Tenebris Umbra ("Dark Shadow" in Latin) Alliance. It wasn't all bad news, as he put it. He also pointed out that this may even bring humanity closer together and stop us fighting amongst themselves. This wasn't exactly my idea of a silver lining. More like a raincloud. Or a hurricane.

A few nights had passed until we got down to the nitty gritty of how we were going to save humanity. The AI on the device he had given me kept me occupied. Occupy meaning ANNOY. The AI Sal was even a bigger asshole than his real counterpart. He would change my playlist, send me pointless abusive messages, drop reception whenever he wanted, he even changed my ringtone to "Everything I Hate About You" by Ugly Kid Joe. When I asked him why he did this, he just responded with "I'm bored and I have nothing better to do". AI Sal even named the phone the sPhone and used Sal Tel to communicate. I really thought an AI would have come up with something better but it fit in with his slightly egotistical ways. I was almost glad when the real Sal would visit.

One visit, he FINALLY told me that what the plan was. He also told me to keep me motivated that he knew exactly where Summer was and he had interfered with the tracking system so she was also safe. He promised that if I helped him to achieve his goal, quickly, he would give me Summer's location and the repopulation of Earth would stop immediately. I also found out that I was not the only person he had approached. There was a scientist called Dr. Joseph Cameron who would be helping me with this project and he would be arriving here tomorrow. Sal was currently helping him navigate his way from Scotland. The plan was this: we would be building a sort of jamming device/ registry collection machine. We had to get the parts and construct it ourselves. Dr. Cameron, who I was told is vastly more intelligent than I am, but in the grand scheme of the universe is still an idiot, was a leading expert in mechanical and electrical engineering. He would be building the device from Sal's plans while I would be scavenging for the items needed. I would then work with him to develop an app that would work on people's smart devices and the new Sphone and would alert them if they were randomly marked. By activating the app, they wouldn't be taken. However, the smart device HAD to be within 2 meters of them and the app activated for it to work. Sal estimated that once built, we could stop the repopulation in about a month. He was unsure what would happen after this but it had to be better than what was happening now.

Chapter XIII - JC

It was about 2:00 p.m. one afternoon and I was lying on the fortress of solitude's floor behind some makeshift sandbags. I had my rifle locked and loaded with the sights pointed towards to the doorway. I had cleared a path directly to the back of the pool down into the sewers and to my escape ladder if needed. Hanging from the ladder was a rucksack with some food, a handgun, ammo and water. There was no noise from outside. The sun was shining and if I wasn't in one of the most dangerous places in the world, I would probably be sitting in the garden having a nice cold cider. My mouth was nearly drooling at the prospect of what could have been. I couldn't stay in this fantasy world forever as I was told that at some point this afternoon, Dr. Joseph Cameron would appear. Sal had told me not bother with precautions but he was responsible for a lot of deaths so I wasn't talking chances. I was also looking forward to having some company as I had suffered so much bloodshed. I was quite worried about letting someone in again but I couldn't do this on my own so I had no choice. I was generally a little bit of an introvert so the prospect of meeting someone new, letting them into my fortress of solitude and saving humanity together was pretty overwhelming. The changing room area had indeed lived up to its name and changed over the past few days. I had set up a bunking area for Dr. Cameron and one of the shower rooms had been cleared to store all of the equipment needed to start the build. Dr. Cameron's help was only to be temporary as we needed a more secure location in case anyone decided to drop by unexpectedly. Sal suggested extending an area under one of the showers and gating it off close to the escape tunnel. The sPhone beeped, "Dr. Cameron is approaching. Say 'Hi' from me, Al Sal, the awesome one."

I had been lying for around 4 hours so this was welcomed news as I was getting bored. I heard someone approaching so I raised my rifle sight to my eye. I clicked off the safety quietly and waited. The plan was to remain perfectly still and not move until the target was within the foyer and I had a clean shot. The footsteps got closer and I could hear someone climbing over the rubble. This was another rudimentary security measure I had put in place. I gathered rubble to put around the road outside to make vehicles detour and people clamber over it creating noise which gave me warning. I saw a shadow and then a man appeared to the left of the doorway. He had his arms raised and per instructions I had given Sal, he used the code phrase "Ezio Auditore" which was a character from Assassin's Creed, one of my favourite games. Man, I've not gamed in a while. He walked into the foyer and I could see a handgun on this hip. He was carrying a large bag on this back. I lay exactly where I had been and pointed the rifle directly at this head. He cleared his throat, "Matthew, I'm unarmed. The passcode is Ezio Auditore" in a very gruff Scottish Accent. I guessed Glasgow from the tone of it. I stayed in my position, "Come towards the ticket barrier with your arms raised and lower your backpack to the floor, toss your handgun to the side and turn around and continue backwards until I say stop", I said as authoritatively as I could. He hesitated and put his arms towards his hip. Then I stood up with a jolt, "KEEP YOUR FUCKING

BACK TOWARDS ME AND WALK BACKWARDS ARM UP. I WILL SHOOT IF YOU DON'T DO AS I SAY". "I WAS REACHING FOR THE BACK PACK RELEASE", he shouted back and I heard him mutter the words "dick head" under his breath. He continued to place his bag down and walked backwards, I swung my rifle over my shoulder and lifted my side arm towards him and cocked it so he could hear it. "Good, now what's your name? Where are you from? Why you here?" I knew all this but I wanted to confirm with him. "My name is Dr. Joseph Cameron. I'm from Glasgow and I'm here due to our mutual friend. Sal. Look, I've travelled 6 days to get here for fucks sake. Will you give me a break?" he said in his Scottish accent sounding ever so slightly pissed off. "Stay there. Do you have any weapons?" I asked as I approached him. "No, just the handgun you noticed", and he lifted his jacket up as he spun around to show me. "I wouldn't come all this way without being armed. The big smoke is a dangerous place at the best of times. I was taking a big risk coming into this foyer without my weapon drawn but Sal told me you are a bit touchy and grumpy and kind of like a caged ape", he chuckled as he said that last bit. I must admit him using Sal's name, my name and also telling me something Sal would have said, relaxed me.

"OK, right, follow me", I said as I lowered my weapon. I still kept it cocked and ready in case anything bad was about to happen but I did offer my hand to shake it. He stood up and dusted himself off and offered his hand towards me, "Look, you don't need that, just put it down", he said softly and calmly as we shook hands. "Sorry, it's just living here in the middle of a military war zone surrounded by aliens and people who want to kill you, makes you a little paranoid so I had to make sure you were who you said you were", I said slightly sheepishly as maybe I had reacted a little. This is when I got my first look at him, he was 6', grey wispy hair on top but still black on the sides, pretty skinny but looked like he did hit the gym as he looked well-built. Also, without shaving for 6 days or so, he was starting to look a little ragged. He was wearing urban combat fatigues and converse trainers which didn't quite go with the overall look. "Follow me", I said as I lead him into the old changing room areas. "Welcome to the fortress of solitude" as I said it, I opened my arms like some cool music was going to play. "That's your bunk there", I pointed to his area. "If you need to shower, we do have water. The toilets are there and cooking facilities are over there and well that's about it for the grand tour." I wasn't going to tell him about the escape routes just yet. I thought this to myself as I put my gun on the rack and gave him a little smile. He hadn't showered for 6 days but thankfully decided to do so while I cooked some food for him. I made him beans and little sausages from an army ration kit I had stolen and we sat chatting for what seemed like a few hours. He had filled me in on what happened outside of London since the Attack.

Surprisingly, the rest of the world went on with life pretty normally. Yes, there were massive travel bans to the UK as it had become a huge no fly zone. New cults surfaced mainly in America to worship the aliens. People had been even volunteering to be taken by the aliens in the repopulation which was now common knowledge around the world. Tension worldwide was still high and most nations were divided on what to do and how to help. Countries like Russia, North Korea and China had forged a new alliance with the sole purpose to communicate with the aliens to try and obtain the new technology; however, little was known about this progress. NATO had grown in size from its original 29 states to 40 with countries such as Brazil, South Korea, Australia and New Zealand joining as they were looking for diplomatic solutions but nothing useful appeared to be coming from it. Sal said that they would not be negotiating at all according the council. The same for the quality of life could not be said for the UK. It was estimated that 30 million residents had sought asylum in various parts of the European Union. There were mass refugee camps around the southeast for those who left London in the initial attack. The value of the British Pound was at its lowest point ever in existence and all of the major UK businesses had either collapsed or were lucky enough to move operations abroad. There was mass poverty, rioting and looting in most areas. All airports below Leeds Bradford had been taken into military ownership and there were very few flights leaving or entering the UK for commercial use. The cost of a seat was £2000 minimum due to the low pound, increased fuel costs and demand. The UK was also currently home to a 500,000 strong military presence from the whole of NATO. Those who hadn't left the UK, were taxed with building massive new development and housing areas in the North of England. But with the lack of jobs and weak pound these places were becoming more like slums than gleaming examples of mass movement.

Dr. Cameron had to travel mainly by night and had abandoned his car near Watford due to the destruction everywhere and lack of any properly functional roads. He had to go on foot the rest of the way which was around 17 miles. He knew that his beloved Volvo S90 was probably never going to be seen again so he had actually taken the Volvo badge as a keepsake and tucked it in his pocket.

I'd decided that I needed to start running around as quickly as possible gathering items and that Dr. Cameron needed to build this device ASAP and not just because Sal promised to find Summer for me and I hadn't had sex in such a long time. OK, maybe that was part of it. Would she even remember me, though? I ran a pretend conversation through my head.
"Hi Summer. Remember me? From the swimming pool?"
"No, sorry", as she raised her gun and shot me in the head.
I was more hoping it would go: "Hi, Summer, remember me? From the swimming pool?"
"OMG YES! Have sex with me now!"
And we lived happily ever after. I mean my heart and dick hoped it would be the latter but to be fair I would be happy not to be shot in the head as I was quite fond of having my head attached to my shoulders.

Before any of this could happen, we needed supplies and my god the list was MASSIVE. Things I hadn't even heard of. Sal said he couldn't supply us with ANY of his technology to make this device but he could help us acquire the items. By "us", he meant me as I would be the one scavenging and hunting down these items. Even though he couldn't supply us with any technology to build it, he said that he would be helping us out greatly with using his technology to acquire the items. He was able to teleport me to locations and even use his cool time stopping technique for me to get some of the more exotic materials. Sal had also supplied me with a suit which acted almost like cloaking technology which would render me nearly invisible to the naked eye. It looked almost like a chemical hazard suit but thinner and all white covered in little sensors and light projectors with a helmet that contained a visor projecting a 360-degree view. It slightly needed adapting from the 7' aliens to my size but with a flick of my wrist, it would project and bend light around the wearer. It was so awesome! I wanted to keep it. The sPhone was now coming in handy and no longer used just to insult me. It had been loaded with the GPS location of EVERYTHING that we needed and was used to communicate anywhere in the world with Sal and Dr. Cameron. Finally, and the most exciting thing that he supplied me with, was an alien stun gun in case we ran into danger. Not only did it stun anyone that I shot at, it also erased the last 15 seconds of their memory. The gun was about the same size as my handgun and was made of some sort of metallic substance that was very light and cold to the touch. There was one button on the handle which enabled it to shoot to a range of around 15 meters.

I was told that in no uncertain terms, was I to use this technology without Sal's approval. He said that the danger not only to himself but to all of humanity if ANY alien technology was found on Earth could result in the whole world being annihilated. So, the stakes were high and acquiring these items would have me traveling to 5 continents, 50 countries and would take around a month of working every night to retrieve some of Earth's rarest materials. This included: Californium 252 of which only 8 grams existed and we needed 1 gram of it; Tritium which I was assured costs around £10 MILLION per pound; Plutonium which is radioactive but used in such areas as powering spacecraft. So, this all sounded fun. By that, I mean it was added danger due to the time zones that I would be entering during the day. Also, on the list was a hazmat suit, solid cold connectors, generators, monitors, signal boosters and all sorts of other things creeping up on over 100 items. Sal had given us instructions to pass off to a chemist named Dr. Henrick Sam who resided in Northern France. His job was to create metals that we hadn't even discovered yet on Earth. I did wonder how many people Sal had been visiting but he assured me that he kept it to a bare minimum. But Dr. Sam was a leading chemist working for the military so he couldn't join us here without causing some major issues and questions. So now, we had the list, we had the means, the time scale and now all we needed to do now was start collecting.

This is where Sal started to get grumpy with me as I decided that the easiest way to keep track of our progress was to give everything names that were easy to understand. I mean, come on, some of things were being created and didn't even exist here yet so they needed a name. Pokémon was a bit of a childhood obsession of mine so everything on the list was given a Pokémon name. The rarest and most challenging things to find had names such as Onix,

Magmar and Ditto. Common items were given names like Eevee, Krabby and Mankey. In the fortress of solitude, we had drawn up a list of every item and where we were going to find it and then we would cross off as we went. Dr. Cameron (now referred to as "JC") would follow the plans and build this device as I scavenged the materials. After 30 days, we should have a completed device that we unanimously decided to call the
"FU machine". Sticking it those aliens was going to feel good. In my down time, Sal said that I had to design the app too which he assured me that he could do most of the more complex coding of which I was unfamiliar. Finally, I would need to hack into the USA military mainframe computer to locate some of the items due to Sal's inability to locate them.

We now had the locations of 96 of the items on the list. But the locations for the last 4 would not be known until I was able to hack the mainframe. This sadly didn't involve any "Mission Impossible" type of hacking as Sal had a device to do it all for us but I still had to physically be beside the mainframe which would require a fair bit of organization. That night, we decided to rest as it was going to be one hell of a complex, tiring and dangerous 30 days. I wanted to start off on a good note so I did what any sensible mature adult would do when faced with this sort of situation. I got drunk with JC, chatted about our favourite video games and passed out.

I was very rudely awakened by JC, I swear, only minutes later. "Wake up, Matthew. It's time to start getting prepped", as he kicked my foot. "Urghhhh", I managed to grumble. I had one hell of a hangover. He kicked my foot again. "I'm up, I'm up", I grunted as he passed me a steaming hot coffee. We decided to name our plan 'Operation Knightmare' after one of my favourite TV shows. It seemed fitting as on this show, a person would guide his friends through a maze filled adventure with many obstacles so it seemed fitting. I always wish that I had been born in the eighties so I could have taken part in this show so now I had my chance. Sort of. We decided that we would start with the easy items first and then move onto the difficult items. By day twenty, we would be going after the hardest items which were the four that we couldn't locate. By day twenty-seven, it should be smooth sailing for me as it was all up to JC then to have this device operational. He would only be coming on a few outings due to the fact that if anything happened to him, the FU machine couldn't be built at all.

We had a few hours to kill before Sal arrived to start Operation Knightmare. I, for one, was very excited as I had become so restless and bored. I decided in all of my wisdom that the time was now to give the invisibility suit a test run. JC was in deep thought looking over information while I lay on the floor bored. We would try to spend a little time apart when we could just to give each other some breathing room as it was pretty cramped quarters now. "Right, I'm just heading for some fresh air", I said as I grabbed the suit without him knowing. "I'll be back in a bit." "OK, see you when you get back", he said without even looking up from this book. With this, I grabbed my rifle and headed outside.

Once I was outside the fortress of solitude, I donned the suit and walked west towards an army checkpoint. I knew this one well as we had stolen supplies and ammo in the past. It was manned by members of four different forces. The sun was about to start setting as I jogged the one kilometre to the checkpoint. I passed a shop that still had part of its glass window intact and did a double. All I could see was a floating gun. "OMG, this is AWESOMEEEEEEE", I said to myself. I couldn't see my own face but if I could, I'm sure it had the biggest smile. The stun gun had camouflage capabilities but unfortunately the energy to camo human tech like my rifle, would take too long to sort according to Sal. I just don't think he wanted to do it to be honest. A few minutes later, I arrived at the checkpoint. I stopped about 200 meters away around a corner and hid my rifle under a pile of rubble and moved forward. I counted six guys all centred around a table playing cards and not one of them was keeping an eye out hence why we had easily raided this place a few times. Very slowly, I walked towards them. 100 meters, 50 meters, 20 meters. I moved to the side and pushed over an ammo crate. They all turned around to look and one of them was looking directly at me. This was the moment of truth. "Go and pick that up, Jones, you're shit at cards anyway and you're the closest", one of them said to a round of laughter. One of the men stood up and walked towards me. 10 meters, 5 meters, 2 meters….. He walked right past me. I could see him glance sideways like he knew something was there but wasn't sure what. He picked up the crate of ammo and headed back to the table. I let them settle back down before moving away then I made my way back to my rifle very slowly so as not to disturb anything. It worked. Just as I bent down to pick up my rifle, a light blue haze formed around me. "Oh fuck. Sal knew."

He teleported us both back to the fortress of solitude where he held me up against with wall without even touching me and I felt paralyzed again. What followed was ten minutes of Sal basically shouting at me and telling me how stupid I was. I felt like I was in front of my headteacher scolding me in class. He actually had a disappointed tone in his voice as he berated, belittled and called me the main idiot of humankind over and over again. He said that if London was giving a reward for epitome of an idiot, I would win without hesitation. I did try and stick up for myself claiming that I needed to know how it worked before going into the field for real but he didn't buy it. He could read my thoughts, after all, and knew that I was scrambling so I just had to ride it out. Once he calmed down and released me from the wall, he did agree that at that the test worked and was mildly convinced we could pull this off instead of the 50/50 chance he had given it previously. When Sal stopped talking altogether, I could hear JC laughing mostly at himself with pride as he had written on a piece cardboard "London's Biggest Idiot" and placed it on my bunk. To further cement the honour, Sal custom made a gif of me with a dunce hat on and wouldn't stop texting it to me for the remainder of the evening.

Chapter XIV - Operation Knightmare

Today was the day that Operation Knightmare was due to commence. In five minutes, a chain of events would start that would hopefully allow humanity to fight back against the aliens and reclaim our planet. I checked and rechecked my kit at least five times and I knew exactly what to do as well. Most of these places would be smash and grab raids so we expected nothing to go wrong. I would be transported in, invisible of course, grab what I needed and transport out. The only difference would be with some of the harder items on the list. I would have to wait until the alarm sensors were hacked by Sal before we could enter. Even when going to Cape Canaveral to grab what I needed, all I was able to see was a grey box room. No time to poke around and look things over. Advanced alien technology made breaking and entering into some of the most secure sites on earth seem rather dull. I imagined what the films like "Gone in 60 Seconds", "Oceans 11", "The Italian Job", "The Usual Suspects" or just any cop drama would have been like had Sal been around. I imagined them going down along the lines of: "Hey we should steal this", bad guy 1. "OK, let's plan", Sal. "Well, that's the months of planning done", mysterious shadow bad guy. 10 seconds later, "Done."

We even got the task completed early and the only remotely fun part was when I had to break into a lab to steal some experimental VR tech in America. I might have had a little go of a new VR Star

Wars game that was in production and it might have been awesome. But of course, if Sal asks, this never happened. I was sad, though, that I had nobody that I could tell about this as it was so great!

I had a cool collection of stuff now in the FoS (Fortress of Solitude) like a hazmat suit. I may have also stolen a few bits and bobs like a space suit, a Chinese samurai sword, various retro gaming machines including a N64 and a Commodore 64 and the best item of all: a 10-foot walking robot that kind of looked like a giraffe from a lab in South Africa. It had four legs and a long neck and was as cool as hell in a matt blank finish. I didn't even know what it was as it didn't exactly have instructions with, I stole it. I mean, borrowed it. For an undisclosed amount of time. But I named it "Gerry" (since it looked like a Giraffe) and it now lived next to my bed as an expensive looking clothes horse. In my defence, I was also instructed to "borrow" more useful things. We had unmanned aerial and ground attack drones for protection, movement and light sensors, claymores and generators as we were going to be drawing WAY more power than we had been to date. The only thing left to do was wait. We were kind of now running a bit behind schedule. It was day 29 and we still weren't done which obviously annoyed Sal a great deal. He couldn't check in with us too much so as not to raise suspicions but would frequently send messages to our Sphones to keep us on course via AI Sal.

The FU Machine was nearing completion so we moved it underground with some help from Sal. We managed to clear a rather large area under the FoS to work on this project. It was a portable protection unit used by the ARMY and was about 20' long by 20' wide with its own filtration system. It had a large metal door that could only be opened from the inside. On one side of the unit was the FU Machine. One the other side, there was Xbox, sofa, beds and canned food just in case we had to stay here for, well, maybe ever. From the outside, the FU Machine looked like just a normal computer with 3 monitors, a VR type of headset for control, an antenna, a large box behind and was attached to a solar powered generator. Guess who was given the job of installing these solar panels high on top of a basically demolished roof? Me. The generator was hooked up to energy cells which could absorb energy during the day and store it at night. We had enough capacity to power the FoS as well as the disguise for what we were really working on down below underground. Sal advised us that once the device was complete, it would overload the grid system in the whole of London and he was very unsure how this would affect things. But he was planning to use this moment to automatically download and install the app needed to stop the relocation. The app was planned to work almost like a trojan horse computer virus. It was programmed to automatically spread to all devices and those connected to the same network. Sal was hopeful that 70% of the Earth's population had some sort of tech to which this could be downloaded. We developed the app so that as soon as it installed, a warning would appear that said: "PLEASE, DO NOT DELETE THIS APP. It is designed to keep you safe from relocation and from the enemies of Earth. Your device MUST stay within 2 meters of you to protect you scramble the transporters and protect you. You will be given a warning if you are selected to be taken and it will automatically disable and jam location scanners used to find you. You MUST acknowledge receipt of this warning to activate the app and you will only have 30 seconds to do it." In the future, we hoped that the device would automatically kick in once you had been selected but for now, this is what we had to work with as we needed to get this out to the wider population as quickly as possible. Sal cautioned me that once we made the app go live, the rest of his council would notice and try and take as many people as possible or maybe even start killing off humans. But he assured me that, chances are, they would cut ties from Earth and run once they realized that humanity was fighting back as no species has ever developed a way to stop them doing what they wanted. Technically we hadn't yet but we had a very annoying yet helpful alien on our side. Those that didn't have the means to download the app were in trouble but we also had managed to install blockers in mobile phone masts and just had to hope that if they didn't have a phone that someone close by them did.

Three days later we were ready to roll. We had set 17:00 p.m. as the time to start the process. Sal would break away from his spaceship convention and join us early. He figured that they would have way too many issues to handle to worry about one rouge alien helping us. The reason that we settled on this time of the evening is this is when most people would be awake still and we could warn them before the full darkness of night set in. We created a short video explaining our actions to the world leaders and asked that they instruct as many people as possible to download the app and

prepare for what may come. Early estimations were that the app worm would take 20 days to infiltrate and install around the globe but London would be fully protected within 6 hours for those who had a phone. The amount of people that had been relocated from London was now VERY small due to the general population not sleeping after 23:00 hours. But we needed to take these measures with the app in case Sal's council moved ahead with the relocation on a larger scale of the entire UK or worse, the world.
It was 16:58 when Sal made his grand appearance and instructed JC to power up the device. We hadn't actually ever powered it up as we were worried about altering the aliens in some way and they would catch wind of our plan and destroy everything that we had done. I had a tablet in my hand which was wired into the device with the go to codes for the app worm. I still wasn't exactly sure what it did but JC and Sal said that I didn't need to know all of the specifics. Only that when it was finished, II would press the button on the tablet and the worm would be unleashed into the general population. One thing that Sal was very worried about was this getting tracked back to us so that's why we chose a secure a place underground housed in a portable army protection building. We installed motion detectors and sensors around the building with CCTV which I could monitor from the tablet if we were required to move quickly. Sal would transport away and we HAD to keep the device safe. If it stopped working, our plan would fail. It needed to remain on 24 hours a day, 7 days a week until every device was connected to the new network and had downloaded the app worldwide. To help with this, we also had our sentry drones. I had been training JC on how to shoot and even covered a little hand to

hand combat. Once the device was powered up, we had 20 days that we had to remain here and protect it with our lives. The underground bunker that we had constructed was easy enough to defend as outsiders would have to come through the sewer or past the sentry bot so we would know of anyone making an uninvited visit. We decided that for the first 24 hours, the bunker would be on lock down and we would be fully kitted out with weapons and body armour.

I looked at the digital display which was on countdown to 17:00, as soon as it changed from 16:59 to 17:00 the screen flickered to life with one simple command. "Proceed" Y/N." JC was wearing the VR goggles and I was watching my tablet monitoring the CCTV and the command to send the worm out.
"Well, here goes nothing", JC said as he moved his hands to the keyboard and pressed the 'Y' key followed by a very slow unsure tap of the enter key. The screens went blank and the images were transferred to the VR headset. "I have full control now", JC said as I could see him typing commands and smiling while he did.
"Everything is initiated, I can keep track of data streams and the worm's progress virtually from here for the moment to make sure it starts as it should." Sal issued the command "Proceed" and a chilled shiver ran down my back as I worried about what was going to happen next. "Proceeding", JC said clearly so he could be heard. The screens flickered back on to display a progress bar which JC had programmed to be a little Sal walking across the screen with each % of completeness. Even though it only took 20 minutes to reach 100%, it seemed to be an eternity and my eyes did not move off the

CCTV feed. I looked over at the monitors and the screen changed to show a 3D map of our immediate area highlighting the distance to the alien ships and in large green matrix type writing were the words "ARE YOU SURE YOU WANT TO PROCEED? Press Y/N."

JC turned in my direction and said, "When I press the 'Y' button, your tablet will display a similar command and then reboot. Once it reboots, you need to confirm the command again and then we can start", his lips curled into an even larger smile as he said this. He didn't seem at all stressed out.

The tablet rebooted and I clicked the 'Y' button, JC sat back in his chair and typed a command and then I saw on screen a red line moving towards the spaceships and a blue circle moving out from this location. JC picked up the motion controllers and followed the red line. On the 2nd monitor were three countdowns. One counting down from 5 minutes and the other two read the number 0. One screen would indicate the number of devices contacted and the other screen would show the number of devices that accepted the app.

The screen showing the devices that had been contacted changed from 0 to 1. I checked my phone; the worm was installing and up popped the warning message that I needed to accept. "It's working", I said, "Exactly as we planned" and I slid my phone back into my pocket. The number 1 was now at 1,000 and climbing with 30% already accepting the app. The red line was getting closer to the alien spaceship. Four minutes later, the red line connected to the alien ships and I am not sure what I was expecting to happen but nothing did.

JC was typing frantically on the keyboard with Sal relaying instructions to him and then I heard what sounded like a massive pulse of energy and I could see something on the CCTV monitor from the camera on the roof that was pointed towards the ships and a brilliant white light emerged and then dissipated. "That's it. You actually managed to pull that off. Maybe are you not as stupid as I thought", Sal said and congratulated JC and myself. "You now have to keep this device safe for 20 days roughly and I will be unable to return in the meantime as I can't risk being found and must lay low for a while. Good luck and AI Sal will take over for me from here" I stopped him, "Aren't you forgetting something?" I asked. " No, I don't believe that I am Matthew", Sal said in that way a fed-up mother may speak to her child. "Hold up now, you need to tell me Summer's location. You promised me, remember?" He sighed, "Matthew, can you just stop thinking about your dick for once in your life? I need your full focus on this. She is alive and well and the worm is already on her device. Until this entire process is complete, you could be putting her in grave danger if you contact her. I have sent her details to your phone but I would highly recommend against contacting her right now because if what we've done is discovered, they will go after her next", and with that he was gone.

"Look, Matthew", JC said in a calming tone as he removed his VR headset, "Sal is right. You don't want her to be brought into all of this. We need to concentrate on saving humanity and on seeing this thing through. We need to protect this device and cannot lose focus now." I took a few seconds to think about things. "You're right JC. She probably won't even remember me anyway", I said as he patted me on the shoulder. I threw myself on the sofa bed, pulled out the Sphone and noticed that AI Sal had changed my background to a party scene. And as promised by Sal, there was a message with Summer's contact details. My finger hovered over it for what seemed like ages. I just wanted to hear her voice and know that she was ok and ask her why she ran away. But then I thought of her safety and decided to close the message, held the phone to my chest and dozed off to sleep.

I wasn't sure how long I had been out but when I awoke, JC was sitting beside me drinking a coffee. "Hey, JC, how long was I out for?", I asked in a slightly gruff voice. He sipped his coffee and looked at his watch, "About six hours, I'd say." "Sorry dude, I just nodded off there. What's the latest?"

"Well, good news all round at the moment. Every mobile device in London has the worm on their phones and from what I can tell, all world leaders have received the video file and are now urging residents to download the app. Well, everyone apart from Russia and China who presumed it was a trick to learn their secrets." "Ah, classic Russia", I thought out loud.

For the next 20 days, it was pretty much a bore fest. We watched the numbers creeping up on the screen and took turns sleeping and monitoring the CCTV and sensors. I'm pretty sure that even the sentry bot was getting bored as I swear that it sighed when I walked past it at some point. But I quickly deduced that I was just going mad from being so bored. I almost wished for some action to find us, even if dangerous, but It never did. If the last 19 were displayed as a montage, it would be increasingly DULL. Mainly just me playing games or moaning about how bored I was and JC sitting there with his headset on worrying about something going wrong. I managed to totally resist the urge to phone or text Summer. One small issue is how much of a weirdo would she think I was that I even had her number. I mean, how do I say, "Hey, I bargained with an alien over the survival of humanity just to get your number?"

It was finally the 20th day when I was startled from an afternoon nap by Sal arriving. As normal, he was his coy self and wouldn't talk about anything apart from what "we needed to know". He advised us that the aliens had indeed tried to expand to the rest of the UK but were blocked as were their attempts to infiltrate the entirety of our planet. Unfortunately, they had discovered our app and had focused efforts intensely on countries that had a low number of mobile devices like Africa, North Korea, Russia and poor countries. They were hit HARD with two more ships landing in South America and Russia. Sal couldn't be 100% positive but he said that roughly 600,000 more humans had been relocated. Because of this, governments were now supplying their residents with mass quantities of cellular devices in hopes to end any further relocating of humans. Overall, Sal said that our efforts were a total success. As he studied the data over the next 10 days, the amount of relocations on average were down. In fact, by FA Day (Fuck the Aliens Day), it was down to 1,000 worldwide per evening. We didn't really celebrate. Most world leaders had contacted us to share their gratitude but no matter what was happening, I just kept thinking of how I've done all of but all I wanted was to contact Summer. I decided that it was time.

Chapter XV - Mam

Using a little bit of alien technology, I discovered that Summer was somewhere in District 2 in what seemed to be a rather large compound with beefed up security including large walls in the middle of what seemed to be a residential street. Luckily, with Sal's tech, getting to her wasn't going to be an issue but the security and her reaction were the unknowns. By now, my name was common place as most people knew that Matthew and JC had saved the Earth. In fact, the President of the United States had invited me to the White House for a formal dinner. Sal transported me there and it was the only time I'd ever been in the States. Nobody knew how we did what we did and with what means or that we were in fact being helped by our resident alien. All communications were handled by AI Sal who had been instructed to be nice and very much unlike his normal self.

Our makeshift bunker had now been significantly reinforced as countries were flocking to help us. We now had such luxuries as aircon, cold food supplies, chemical toilets and a blast door that Sal said even a bomb couldn't scratch. These newfound luxuries were nice as we were basically going to have to stay here for a long time. I hadn't even left the bunker for 10 days as we were now at a war of attrition and had to keep the device going as long as the aliens remained on Earth. Once they decided to piss off, it would be ok but until then, it was almost like a stare down. Who would hold their ground longer without blinking? Us or them? Now that people were becoming more confident and familiar with the system we put in place, life was somewhat returning to normal. I began trying to think of ways to "accidentally" bump into Summer again when Sal materialized into the bunker. "Right, Matthew, I've been in Summer' compound and have seen her", he said way too casually. "Like, what the fuck, Sal? Why? How? What did you see?", I blurted out with a mixture of anger and jealousy. "Well, I may have streamed a fake news story to her phone with your picture in to see what she would do and how she would react. I am quite honestly so tired of you going on about some girl who left you by a swimming pool." JC nodded in agreement at this comment. "And?", I said as I threw a ball of paper at JC. "Well", Sal continued, "The good news is that she recognized you." I cheered a little but then he continued making it worse, "The bad news, before your tiny little brain explodes with excitement, is she wasn't alone." "What, do you mean?", I snapped. "What do you humans say? Having "sex"? She wasn't clothed and was doing strange things with a man.""SHUT UP, SAL!", I shouted. "Yes, Matthew, they seemed physically linked", Sal said. "Fuck", I said as I slumped into my chair and closed my eyes the one thing that I was looking forward to after all of this crap, that little bit of a shining light just had a massive raincloud dumped over it. "Well, this was just like high school all over again", I said. JC stood up and patted me on the shoulder. "Want a tea or something stronger?", he asked. I didn't answer. I was deflated just like I had been punched in the gut and had the wind knocked out of me. I had been searching for her but here she had a boyfriend and never even gave me a second thought. I felt quite stupid that I had gone on about her so like I meant anything to her at all.

The next morning, Sal gave me good news. He managed to locate my mam and decided I could do with something good for a change. Unbeknownst to me, JC and Sal had been tracking her down all night to try and get me out of this mood I was in. For an asshole of an alien, Sal did have a good side so I decided to contact her. It had been such a long time and I guessed she presumed that I was dead by now. But with my face plastered everywhere at the moment, I was hoping she would have seen me and wouldn't be as shocked to hear from me. "The number is programmed in your phone", JC said as he handed it back to me. "How do you feel?" I didn't really know how to feel. I was delighted to know that she was still alive and I could do with a friendly voice right now. "Yeah, I don't know. This is going to be weird as it's been years since we last spoke", I said as blankly looked across the room. "I know, Matt, but by what I can tell, she tried to make it to London to get you but was caught up in worst of it and forced back. I am sure she will be so glad to hear from you. One thing though, Matthew, you HAVE to keep the call short and you are going to have to be careful. I know I sound a little paranoid but we've made a lot of friends out of what we've done but also a lot of enemies."

I headed to the other side of the bunker. The level of privacy in here was low to say the least but JC started listening to some music and put his headphones on to give me what space that he could. I

appreciated the gesture and dialled my mam's number. It rang 4 times. "Hello", said a distant voice.
"Hello? Hello. Who is this?" she repeated. "Hey, mam, it's me, Matthew." I'm not sure why I added "Matthew" after addressing her as my mam as I would hope she would know her own son's voice. The line was silent. Then all I could hear was crying. After a few minutes, the sobbing stopped. "Matthew, I thought I lost you. I mourned for you. I even had a memorial service for you with Jon's and Ross's parents. Then a few years later, I saw your face appearing on the news saying you are responsible for saving humanity. I mean what the FUCK?", she said still sobbing. I had never heard my mam swear. It was like an unwritten rule that mams didn't swear. "I know, I know", I said in that slightly sheepish way that kids do. "You could have just called me, written to me, anything to let me know you were alive." But I couldn't have just called given how we hiding. I didn't have a phone until Sal showed up. I couldn't write as what postman was delivering now? I almost launched into a story of how many times I've been almost killed, the way I've seen my friends die or how for the past 3 months, I've been holed up underground off grid trying to save humanity. Instead, all I did was answer with, "I'm sorry it took me so long to call. I can't talk for long but I will call you tomorrow at the same time. It might be worthwhile going somewhere safe if you aren't already." She sighed, "Safe? Why would I need to go somewhere safe? I have actually moved in with." I interrupted, "Stop, don't say where you are just trust me ok? I've got to go, man. Bye. I love you." "I love you, too, Matthew", and with that I hung up. Over the next few days, I started filling my mam in with all of the news that I'd not

shared yet. She had also been through a lot after 'losing' her son. The family had pretty much drifted apart. Her sister had moved to the relative safety of America. Most of her friends had moved away or left the UK. She asked me to call Ross's and Jon's parents to talk to them and explain to them what I shared with her. I did and they were grateful for the information and felt like they now had proper closer as they actually knew what had happened. It was nice getting back in touch with my mam and having that support and friendly voice. It was really helping to lift the cloud of anxiety that had taken control of me lately. I just really wish I could visit her and give her a giant hug but Sal declined this idea as the level of danger to her was too great. During a conversation one night, she gave me the best advice about Summer. She told me to just do what she did with dad and that was to 'accidentally' bump into her somewhere and play the ignorance card and hope it worked. Worse care scenario, she would dismiss me which, at this point in time, wouldn't make any difference. So, this is what I decided to do. I was going to watch where she was going without her knowing, "bump" into her and see if anything happened.

Chapter XVI - The Factory

After monitoring Summer's movements for a few weeks, I noticed that every Wednesday was her turn for the supply runs. My plan was coming together. With London now coming under somewhat of a new normality, this was going to be a little easier with less of a chance of getting shot in the head. People had generally on the whole stopped shooting and robbing each other. Two thousand military personnel stood down from active duties and were now in partnership the new Metropolitan Police. The MP's numbers were once over 30,000 before the relocation and were now only roughly 4,000 as most had died, left or were relocated. There wasn't much left for them to patrol in so they equipped some old trucks "Mad Max" style but they were now united and all of them were armed. They started putting curfews in place, shutting down illegal operations and the sentencing that they handed out was tough. There was a total crack down on disorder. Districts X and Y were still highly militarized and a no-go zone. Not even the police could enter there. This was mainly because there were still two massive spaceships sitting there but aid was flooding in, shops were starting to reopen, army and civilian engineers were clearing rubble and rebuilding roads and even some schools had reopened. Progress was slow in parts and District 2, where Summer lived, was still one of the most dangerous places to travel. But they had full power and water restored and rubble was being cleared so it was becoming easier for them to move about. People were starting to actually move back into London and the DMZ (the old

M25) was opened up and people could freely move in and out now. I sadly had to stop my mam from coming to see me for me and I told her that it was best for her to remain in hiding for now. In relation to myself and JC, we were still in the bunker and didn't leave very often at all. But the sacrifice was worth it as nobody had been relocated now for weeks. I was excited and shocked to discover that I was nominated for the Nobel Peace Prize but Sal warned me that some of the council members had grown suspicious and started scanning the area looking for our equipment. He noted scouts starting to make regular trips to the surface. We had to be even more careful now. We just had to win this war of cat and mouse and then hopefully we could leave our bunker and return to normal life. But our bunker was well defended and hidden. Even if JC and I died, the device should be able to operate for another year with no problems. If we were no longer around, Al Sal informed us that he would just get two monkeys to sit in for us and call it good.

It was now Wednesday and in about half an hour, Summer would be leaving for her supply run to a local shop. She always went alone which was unusual as none of the other six people living in her compound seemed to bother. In fact, she wouldn't be there much longer as security forces were clearing compounds so eventually, they would come for her but I was uncertain if she knew this yet. Sal was very reluctant to teleport me over there but with some persuasion and lots of begging, he eventually gave in. He teleported me behind the shop that she was going to enter just before Summer was due to arrive. It felt strange for me to start worrying about something again as I had felt so safe for so long. I carried only my side arm as the NLPF had banned the open carrying of automatic firearms but doing this brought the murder rate of New London now. I was standing near the shop window at this point looking out over a grassy area. It drizzling slightly and people milled about on the streets. I propped my foot up against the wall to try and look somewhat cool. I was dressed in the smartest jeans and t-shirt that I had, wearing a black NYY cap and had even shaved my beard down a bit to try and look smart. I then looked to my right and there she was. I hadn't seen her up close since that fateful night that the world changed forever. She looked as beautiful as ever but now had the look of someone who had seen it all. Like a lot of people, her humanity had been taken. I wondered about what she had been through and how she survived. I would hopefully be able to find that out. I'm not the best to think up plans so I decided that I was going to do the 'accidentally' drop something in front of her routine followed by "Oh, hey! Do I know you?" I had seen this work in many films so it had to work for me or else I would look like a total dick. She was now barely 10 meters away from me and I just couldn't help but stare at her. She was beautiful. But my illusion of a happy romantic comedy was very quickly ruined. "What the fuck are what you looking at?", she snapped at me as she approached. I was taken back, "Erm, sorry." I just looked down at the ground sheepishly but continued, "It's just that you look familiar so I was trying to work it out is all." I was now wishing that the ground would just swallow me up. Summer looked me up and down, "Sorry, mate. No, I don't know you", and she walked past me. I felt like the geek in class who was been dismissed by the high school football star or something. "Sorry", I looked up and met her glaze. I stepped back towards the

window as she walked into the shop. "Well, I fucked that up", I muttered under my breath and too started to walk away. "Matthew?!", I heard a voice. I didn't turn around as I guessed it was just my imagination. "Matthew, you're Matthew, aren't you? The guy from the television? And from the swimming pool? I realised it as soon as I got into the shop", she said in a much less harsh tone now. "Yeah, that's me. Hey, Summer." "Look, I'm sorry for acting like a bitch. You know what it's like around here during these times." At this point, I wanted to do a happy dance, jump in the hair and click my heels but I decided to play it cool instead. "You remember the swimming pool, huh?", I tried to keep the big beaming smile off my face. Ah, she remembered me.
"Yeah, how could I forget? You saved my life." "And you, mine", I replied. "So, how come you are here?" she asked. This is the question that I had been dreading as I knew I would have to lie. "Well, this was my old neighbourhood." Lie number one. "I was just seeing if my friend was about as he lives", I picked a random direction, "Over there." Lie number two. "I was just going to stop by this shop to pick up some supplies before heading over." Meh, this was one half true. She raised one eyebrow like she thought I was full of shit. "Well, it was good to see you, Matthew. Maybe I'll see you around sometime? Look, I need to get back to my friends otherwise they will wonder where I am so here's my number." What I couldn't tell her was that I already had her number but what the hell, I pretended to put it in my phone. "I'll drop you a text or something later", I said like a needy school kid with a crush and with that, she walked back into the shop. Sal gave me a curfew to meet him so that he could teleport me back to the bunker. I know that I

walked with an extra spring in my step but I could swear that I floated to our rendezvous point.

The next few nights, Summer and I talked quite a bit. We discussed experiences that we had survived. I thought that I had it tough but what Summer had been through was even tougher. She brought a ray of sunshine into my life. I was walking around whistling and smiling. I couldn't sleep but not because of anxiety and depression but because I was just so happy. She still hadn't told me that she had a boyfriend yet but when I eventually asked, she was truthful but said that it hadn't been going well lately. Was I a bad person that I celebrated that fact? We decided to meet up in person. I had to explain that I was in hiding so it had to be in a less public area this time as I couldn't risk it. So, we agreed to meet at an old abandoned factory on the outskirts of District 2. I arrived 30 minutes before we were due to meet. The factory was an old processing plant that hadn't seen any action for a while as there was dust everywhere. Coffee cups sat on tables like they were just left there yesterday. Pigeons moved in and the silence of the building was only broken when a pigeon flapped its wings. Light streamed through the massive windows as I stood there and I could feel the sun on my face. It was nice after mainly living in the bunker these days. The factory was massive and over 3 floors high. I guessed it was built in the 1930's due to the layout and décor. It was mostly intact with no smashed windows and no graffiti. I don't think anyone had been in here since the doors shut. My phone rang and it was Summer. "Hey, Summer." I had asked her to call me on approach just so I knew that it was her who was approaching. "I'm just outside the gates so

don't shoot me", she almost nervously laughed. "I won't", I chuckled, "See you in a minute". For security, I had bought a drone so I could actually see her approaching on my phone app. Once I confirmed it was her and that she was alone, I set the drone to a patrol pattern and stood in the middle of the room. The sun was beaming through the glass and dust particles could be seen floating in the air. As she walked towards me, she looked like an angel as she broke each beam of light. "You know how to treat a girl huh, Matthew?", as she gave me a hug and kiss on the cheek. "Well, you know I've not had much practice with girls as I've been busy saving the world and what not." This reply received a playful punch on the arm from her. We walked towards one of the main offices. I had brought a little picnic and laid down a rug in there. This gesture was well received. We ate some nice food, had some wine and chatted for hour. At one point, she leaned in to kiss me. To say that I had butterflies floating about inside was an understatement. And my God, did I get hard quick which was kind of embarrassing when she looked down and saw it poking up from my jeans. I looked sheepishly at her.
"Ah, what the hell, we could die tomorrow", and she gently laid me back and started kissing me passionately. She undid my trousers and pulled down my underwear. "This seems a bit one sided", I said so I started to take her top off and unhook her bra. Wow, she still had an amazing body. She moved my hands up onto her breasts. They were firm and perfect just as I had imagined. She undid her trousers and slid them off as she started to kiss down my body. Her lips were soft and my excitement levels rose. After years of 'alone time', dreaming of this night and having the most gorgeous

wonderful girl in my arms, I didn't last long. It was amazing and afterwards we lay there the rest of the night wrapped in the picnic blanket kissing, talking and generally acting like two teenagers in love. But as usual in New London, bad news was always just around the corner.

Chapter XVII - Russians

A few days passed and communication between Summer and I was limited. She was now feeling slightly guilty for what she had done since she still had a boyfriend. I still felt on top of the world even though I think I was being slightly ghosted by her. The days after our embrace, I felt like Julie Andrews in the "Sound of Music" dancing and singing on top of a lush green hill. Just replace lush green with grey and hill with bunker and singing with being told to shut up by JC constantly but same. JC and I were sitting in the bunker having one of our usual "Would you rather?" conversations. These happened at least once a week and always kept us busy for a bit. Current string of questions:

Would you rather….
Have a finger for a tongue or have tongues for fingers?
Wear someone's dirty underwear or use someone else's toothbrush?
Only be able to whisper everything or shout everything?
Give up sex forever or your favourite food?
Be alone for the rest of your life or surrounded by annoying people?

When I asked the last question, JC kind of give me a look like "Well you're annoying so I guess I should choose that". I did wonder if that's what I had become lately but I wasn't bothered enough by it to change. We played for about another twenty minutes or so when an alarm sounded and an icon appeared on my sPhone. The alarm was coming from one of our surveillance drones above Summer's compound. It had detected gunfire. I tapped the flashing warning triangle on my phone and quickly switched to the camera mounted below the drone. The picture was clear and had Night Vision and Heat Signature capabilities. It was now dusk and there was a smog in the air from a nearby burning building. I switched to night vision mode, the screen went green and I took the drone off patrol mode. I lifted it higher into the air in order to get the full picture of what was happening. I had JC contact Summer. I could see tracer rounds streaking across the yard towards the compound gate followed by a large explosion which ripped a hole through the main house. JC passed me phone. "Matthew!", she shouted over the sound of automatic gun fire. "Summer, the drone is picking up five heavily armed people moving towards the main gate so concentrate your fire there", I said as I moved the camera in to Summer's location. "Understood, Matthew, I'm really worried. We are quite low on ammo and we were not ready for this." "Just hold up there as long as you can and keep the place secure and stay safe. I will think of something. Just stay on the line", I said trying to remain calm. A message appeared on my phone from AI Sal saying he had contacted Sal and he would be on the line in a second. "Matthew, this is bad. My intel shows these men are Russian special forces and we have been monitoring their movements for some time but were not expecting them to strike like this. They somehow know that Summer is linked to you. They have tried to get close to your mother but were unable to track her down, thankfully. I was able to wipe some of their data by planting a Sal worm in a laptop they had and hid the information about your mother but there was nothing that I could do about Summer's compound due to the proximity. More bad news, it seems the council have come up with an agreement with the Russians and I'm unable to find out any more information other than that the world might not be as safe as we thought! This is only the beginning." "FUCKING HELL! Right, one problem at a time", I shouted as I headed to the lockers to grab my gear. "Look, just get me over there, Sal. I'm going to suit up now and get Summer out of there." "Matthew, I can't do that", Sal said. "We will be vastly compromised and run a real risk to ourselves and so many other lives if you go out there." "Look, it's fucking happening now. JC keep me updated on the situation and Sal be prepared to transport me. We go in, help out, if nothing can be done then you transport me straight back and we deal with any issues. JC, inform Summer that I am coming and if I don't return...." I never finished my sentence as I ran to the locker area. I picked up my assault rifle, attached a torch on the under-barre, put on my tactical vest, some NV goggles, picked up my throat mic, 3 clips of ammo and 2 frag grenades, my trusty sidearm and a med kit. "Right, Sal. I'm ready. Get me over there" and with a flash I appeared to the rear of Sumer's building.

It was pitch black by now but the noise was intense. Automatic gunfire and explosions were all around. I pressed my throat mic, "JC assess the situation for me and locate Summer" I implored as I ran into the first floor of the building. JC responded immediately, "We have 1 attacker injured and 2 defenders. One confirmed KIA. Summer is located 1 floor above you and is aware you are there but confused at how you arrived. Sal is ready to transport you back as soon as you give the go ahead. You need to exit the room you are currently in, go up the stairs to your left and turn right but be careful. Russian forces are in the compound and advancing quickly. The drone is switched to heat mode so I can track every movement." "Received, JC. See you soon, I hope. Over" and ended the transmission. I slung my assault rifle over my shoulder and drew my pistol, I turned the safety off and put my NV goggles down, opening the door and covered my angles as best as possible and moved towards the stairs. I heard a large explosion near me and Russian commands shouting. I had no idea what they were saying but I knew that I had to move quickly. The Russian outfits were armed with the AN-94 which had a 60 round capacity mag and limited to Russian Special forces. It could fire bursts or full auto with an 1800 RPM mode. There was way that I wanted to be on the receiving end of that. I moved quickly up the stairs and to the door to which Summer was behind. I could hear footsteps behind me. I tried the door handle and 5 rounds flew through the door just narrowly missing my head. "It's me! Matthew! Stop firing! We don't have much time", the footsteps were getting closer as I heard shouting and a few more rounds of gunfire followed by a scream. JC came over the network, "Make that 2 KIA from the defenders." I heard the door unlock and Summer dragged me into the room. We quickly locked the door. Inside the room was a very bemused Summer, her boyfriend who shouted "Andrew" and another male shouted "George". They were down to their last 2 clips of ammunition. We had 4 very heavily armed Russian Special forces on their way. I filled them in quickly on the situation and grabbed Summer's arm moving her behind some cover. "Andrew, you and George take up defensive positions and block the door if you can." I threw Andrew my assault rifle and ammo. There was no way that we could defend our position so I decided that running was the only option for Summer and I. In a very selfish move, I decided that I could only rescue her and I. Andrew and George moved up towards

the door and started putting boxes in front of it. I knew there was little hope they would survive. What the fuck had I become? Had I lost all of my humanity as I was willing to sacrifice two human lives for the sake of getting Summer out of here?
"They have cleared the floor before you and they will be coming up within seconds", JC said over the radio. I grabbed Summer's arm as she tried to go help Andrew. "Summer, stop. I can't explain what's about to happen. Just trust me ok? All will become clear and will be OK", I could hear JC counting down when there was an almighty explosion. Andrew and George were caught right in the middle of it. Pieces of them flew across the room and the sound was unreal. A fire ball raced towards us. I didn't even have to utter the words and the blue bubble appeared around us. Everything outside of the bubble stopped. The flames coming towards us, the rounds of gunfire zipping through the air, the room bright with colour. It all stopped. All I could hear was Summer screaming for Andrew as she looked into my eyes, I saw her pain. Then a split second later, we were in the bunker.

She held onto me crying and screaming for what seemed like hours afterward. I didn't know what to say or do so I just held onto her. I held her closer than I had ever held anyone else and just kept whispering in her ear that it was going to be OK. JC put a blanket around her and when I tried to tuck it in close, she pushed me away. She laid in a ball for the rest of the night and eventually cried herself to sleep.

Chapter XVIII - New London

In the morning, I checked on Summer who was just sitting there staring at the wall. She wasn't crying now but an eerie silence had fallen over the bunker. Nobody quite knew what to say. JC just sat at the computer awkwardly as he didn't know what to do. After about an hour of complete silence, I decided to say something as I always had to fill silence with pointless conversation. I walked over and sat on the floor beside Summer. "Hey, how you feeling?", I asked with instant regret. She had just watched her boyfriend being blown to bits, her home was destroyed and she was teleported to a secret underground bunker. I mean what could she say. "I guess I'm in one piece but I think you have some explaining to do", she said without ever diverting her gaze away from the wall.

I told her the whole truth with no detail left unturned. As soon as I mentioned Sal, she looked at me for the first time and I think that was the point that she realized this was bigger than she ever thought. She couldn't meet Sal until later as I wanted trying to give her some time to adjust. Finally, she and JC had a bit of a chat too. I got her some proper food and a hot cup of tea. After a few hours, she was still distorted but I could see a bit of a glint in her eye and the odd flicker of a smile when JC and I were carrying on as we normally did. What I hadn't told Summer yet was where we were. I thought it might be better to show her as this was the place, we first met all those years ago. I decided that it might also do JC some good to get out of the bunker for a bit, too.

We had drones above the old swimming pool, sensors on the ground and sentry guns positioned in key locations so I felt pretty confident we would be fine. We left the bunker entrance and went

up the stairs to the locker room. JC went up first with his assault rifle in hand to scout the way. He gave us the all clear so we stepped up. "I'll give you some space", JC said as he went out towards the lobby and outside for the first time. I am sure I could hear him inhaling the fresh air as he went.
"So, do you recognise the place?", I turned to Summer and smiled. There was a moment silence.
"OMG, it's the swimming pool! What the fuck?", she gasped. "Yeah, I returned here and set up. Once I lost my friends, I figured what else did I have to lose? And yeah, that's where you left me to die after dragging me out of the pool", I pointed and jokingly tried to lighten the mood a bit.
"I regret that decision but I was scared, Matthew. I had no idea what to do. I dragged you out and left you as best as I could and just ran. I didn't stop running Matthew", and she held me and just cried. I held her tightly, kissing her head and stroking her hair. JC came running back in, "I'm pretty sure I just saw something out there. I'm worried that we are compromised but the drones are not picking up anything. What I saw kind of looked like Sal but taller." "Well it was nice while it lasted", I said and we went back down to the bunker immediately sealing the door and activating all security measures. Right on que, almost no sooner than we had closed the door, Sal appeared. And a very surprised Summer drew her side arm and pointed it towards him. "Whoa, whoa, whoa, he's with us", I said with my hands making the international symbol for calm the fuck down. "That's Sal. Remember the friendly but slightly asshole alien that helped us?" And with that, she lowered the gun. "I would say it's nice to meet you, Summer, but you pointed a gun at me. You humans seem all of the same to me but after spending most of my time with these two buffoons, it might be nice to have some sort of half intelligent conversation with someone else ", quipped Sal.

"See? I told you he was an asshole", I said as we laughed. I'm sure if Sal could have, at this point I would've received a middle finger.

"Anyway", he continued, "The situation is much worse than we expected. JC, you did indeed see another council member outside. They have been appearing all over the city. So far nothing has happened apart from scaring the locals. As far as I can tell, they are just floating there as a last-ditch attempt. If you look on the monitor", he zoomed in on the image, "This is about 2 miles from our current location." Sure enough, just hovering there in a street corner was a dark shadow of a featureless body and glowing white eyes. "As far as I can tell, this is a new tactic of theirs. They move from location to location within a mile radius every hour or so. I am unsure why, Matthew, but this is worrisome to me as I have never seen this sort of behaviour before." "Um this is worrying? What about the Russians who attacked Summer's compound?" I asked him. "Before I talk about this, I have more news." I'm sure if he had a face, he would look worried right now. "The scientist we used to create some of the materials that we needed was found dead this morning in his apartment. No CCTV and we didn't have a drone there as we thought he was safe in his undisclosed location. I don't know who did it but if I had to guess, I would say the Russians." "Fuck", JC and I said almost in unison. "I have tracked some to Newcastle so I would suggest that you contact your mother and move her somewhere safe as a priority. Also, the bunker needs to remain in total lock down from now on. Anyone approaching will be considered a threat. This will also be my last visit. We have to hope that this is a final roll of the dice from the council and we can win the war of attrition. We can keep in contact with AI Sal as that is fully untraceable by them but the teleporting can be detected so that has to stop", and with that he vanished. No goodbye. Nothing. I thought it was fitting for him just to vanish. I was always surprised with how much time he chose to spend with us as it was.

Once Sal left, JC decided to drop a bombshell. He wanted to leave and return home. I could tell he was starting to think three was a crowd in the small bunker and now his job was pretty limited. He did what needed to be done. He had been in New London for a long time. He even offered to take my mam with him and offer her protection which she was happy to agree to. I think she fancied him a bit to be honest and I shuddered at the thought. He had nothing here. His car was still hopefully parked where he left it and now that the streets were a little more crowded and patrols were stepping down, hopefully he would make it ok. And 12 hours later, he was packed up and said his goodbyes.

In the span of 24 hours, JC and Sal were gone. But I was hoping that JC would be with my mam within 12 hours then they'd both be on to safety soon after that. We did deploy a drone to monitor JC until he left New London and we could see that he made it out with no problems and his car was exactly where he left it. Now it was just Summer and I in the bunker but at least we were safe.

Chapter XIX - New Zealand

The next few weeks were strange to say the least. Summer and I were under total lock down, my mam and JC were safe just north of Stirling in Scotland and life in New London was really starting to return to normal once again apart from many reports of "aliens" lurking around. Oddly, they never did anything. Just lurked about. And there had been no sign of the Russians anywhere. We did have a few issues with people moving back into area around here. On one occasion, a drone almost killed a child who had wandered into the pool area. Security was becoming a huge problem for us with the population of New London getting bigger and bigger every passing day. It wouldn't be long before someone would stumble across the bunker or get taken out by a drone. Or both.

Then it happened. Three weeks after JC left, I was awakened by a LARGE tremor. It was about 3:00 a.m. Summer was already grabbing her sidearm as I was reaching for my rifle. We rolled out of bed and Summer ran to the security monitors which were all totally clear. The noise got louder and the ground shook violently causing things to fall over. The roof crumbled. "I'm not seeing anything, Matthew, in our proximity", Summer said while putting a t-shirt over her naked body. I couldn't help but notice that she was remarkably quick at putting clothes on and her breasts looked amazing in the tight t-shirt. "Right", I said as I struggled with a trouser leg and almost tipped over. I took control of one of the high-flying aerial coverage drones and panned it around. "Holy Shit", Summer said as she saw exactly what I saw. Where the three vessels were, there was now a cloud of smoke and debris as they started to lift off of the ground. I zoomed in with the camera. The scaffolding, tents, sheet plastic was all falling off as they rose into the air and with an almighty blinding flash, they vanished.

I couldn't do anything at this moment but hug Summer. It was over, wasn't it? I thought to myself. Just then, I heard my phone beep from the other end of the bunker so I ran over and checked it.
It was a massage from Sal it read: "I don't know if this will reach you in time before we depart but humanity has won and we are leaving your planet. I will probably never see you again. Our home planet is in the Canis Major Overdensity approximately 30,000 light years away. I have passed as much technical data onto your government as I could without being caught in hopes to keep your planet safe in the future. Good luck, Matthew."

For the rest of the day, I just sat there. What a living hell we endured for so long. Millions of lives lost, ruined or relocated. London basically destroyed, my friends were all dead but somehow, I survived, helped save humanity and met Summer. She was the love of my life. I wondered if life would ever fully return back to normal. Would I move back home? Could I start a new life down here? I daydreamed about the possibilities, the hope, the future, my dreams. The next week passed in a blur for Summer and I. We talked until the early hours and mourned lost friends and family. And of course, had a HELL of a lot of sex. Two horny young adults locked in a bunker with nothing to do? Only seemed right. There wasn't a surface of this bunker that we hadn't had sex on. Good thing that JC wasn't here. We shut down the computer system and closed the app down. That should help with any cyber security issues. However, we kept the drones, CCTV and communication side of the program open for the foreseeable future. We passed all of the data that we had over to the UK government in case anything like this were ever to happen again.

New London was starting to party. There were parades, street parties, celebrations rang out from every corner. It was truly amazing. We even managed to attend a few, too. New London was becoming the place to be. Banners and balloons were everywhere. But not just here. The entire world was celebrating our success and the battle won against the aliens. Earth won. We decided that we would move from the UK as we didn't know who was after us still. A new life in New Zealand sounded perfect. Summer's grandad lived there and the land was cheap. Luckily, money wasn't an issue. I had a stashed bank account with over £22 million in it. I had a super smart alien friend and a few countries giving us money and it's not like I could spend it online shopping or anything. I had already donated £3 million to a fund to help children who had been left homeless or left as orphans. This fund was set up anonymously so that no one could trace it back to me. It was linked through several different countries and so far, it was doing a lot of good. I also planned to help out hurting families like my deceased friend's families once I was relocated. I was not just rich in money now I also felt rich in love. Summer showed a level of love towards me that I didn't think was possible. We received an invitation to attend a special ceremony in Zurich hosted by the UN to recognize what I had achieved. I was asked to give a full debrief of everything I knew. I decided that this would be my first and my last public appearance that I would make before we moved to New Zealand. The spotlight was a place that I did not intend to be and I wanted us to start our life together.

Chapter XX - Red Dress

"Right, let's go through this one more time", Summer said as she straightened up my bow tie, "Do you have your speech, spare clothes, passport and money?" I checked my pockets. My speech was in my breast pocket and I could feel it. On the floor was an overnight bag with everything else in it. "Yes, all checked and accounted for." I was wearing a smart tuxedo with a black bow tie and Summer looked beautiful wearing a figure hugging, red sparkly dress which flowed along the floor behind her and red sparkly heels. She was the most stunning woman ever and I felt that she put me to shame. I reached down and picked up the printed email from the table and checked my watch. It was now 2:30 p.m. We wandered into the foyer of the old swimming pool and grabbed our coats and a suitcase. I looked at the email in my hand. It was an itinerary list provided by the British Army who would be escorting us to the airfield. We had still not given our location to anyone but in the weeks following the alien's departure, we had basically cleared the bunker out and shipped the items that we needed to New Zealand. The bunker was rigged with a small explosion which would cause the full collapse of the building once we left. We were not coming back. I would miss this old place when we left but we also had to make sure that nobody knew where we would be living. I glanced behind me and all of the sentry guns had been removed. All of the walls and floors had been bleached and cleaned to clear away as much DNA as possible. It was now just back to an old, ruined, rundown swimming pool building and soon to be a pile of rubble. Summer turned to me, "Matthew, this is where we first met. It's a shame that we will never see it again", she said with a tinge of sadness. I turned to her and held her hand, "I know but we are heading to New Zealand babyyyyyy", and I hugged and I looked into her eyes. We both smiled as we thought about the safety and the warmth of New Zealand.

I checked my communication device; Al Sal was still on here and he had put a sick emoji on screen with the words "Get a room FFS". He would be monitoring the two drones that we had kept behind. One was assigned to keep over watch of the building to make sure that the demolition went according to plan and the other would track us at a distance until we reached the airport. This drone was armed; however, once it followed us to safety, it was tasked to fly into the sea and self-destruct.

Looking down at the email in my hand, it read:

1) Pick up at location A (TBC) at 1500 hrs, full escort provided (No details given)
2) Escort to RAF Northolt – Approx. time 20 minutes
3) Board an US NAVY Osprey
4) 3-hour escorted flight to Geneva Airport, with US Navy Seals
5) Swiss Army to escort to UNOG – Approx. time 10 minutes

After this, we would be escorted back to Zurich to board a private jet and a flight to New Zealand and once there, we would disappear forever. At 14:59 hours, my device alerted me that the 500-yard exclusion zone had been breached. A warning popped up on the screen but since I could hear diesel engines and the distinctive sound of an Army Chinook Helicopter drawing close, I decided to ignore the warning and step towards the main doors. Once outside, I could see the front of the convoy approaching. It consisted of 3 Mastiff PMVs (Protected Mobility Vehicle), 3 Foxhounds and 2 Warrior AFVs (Armoured Fighting Vehicles) plus 1 chinook and 2 Lynx escort helicopters. This was the first time that I had been outside and unarmed since that fateful day so many years ago. It felt good but wrong in some ways. The lead vehicles passed us and the 3rd Foxhound stopped directly in front of us. Soldiers from the rest of the vehicles all jumped out and set up a perimeter. I could almost hear the yelling of instructions over the noisy rotor blades of the helicopter above. A man dressed impeccably smart stepped out of the rear of the vehicle and extended his hand. "Hi, Matthew, my name is Coronal Alexandra and I am here to escort you to RAF Northolt. If you could just follow me. I'm sorry that we couldn't find something nicer for you to travel in, ma'am", he looked towards Summer. He directed us towards the back of the foxhound. Once the door closed, I could see the soldiers heading back to their vehicles and the convoy moved off.

The entire journey was without incident. It was very weird to see people now just going about their daily business. We passed people along the way that seemed to be headed to school. We saw massive buildings being repaired. The streets were busy with buses, taxis, people walking along the sidewalks with shopping bags. It was pretty amazing to think of how much had changed in such a short period of time. The journey was also pretty comfortable with the Coronal preparing us for the next phase. We reached RAF Northolt in the 20 minutes that was expected which was impressive. Even though life was returning to normal, there were still A LOT less people in New London. RAF Northolt had been a main staging post for the past few years and was a mess. There were tents, shipping containers, various military vehicles from around the world ranging from the American HUMVEE to South Korean Battle tanks all lined up on the side of the roads. Every inch of space seemed to have either been occupied or turned into a makeshift road. Even one of the runways was now just a storage area for equipment. There was a rather large hustle and bustle of people as we approached the helicopter landing pad which was just off from the main terminal building. As we drew close the Chinook, 2 Lynx helicopters landed beside what appeared to be a taxi way leading to the runway. Our convoy stopped beside the Osprey. Once again, all of the soldiers jumped out and created a perimeter around the landing site. We were then escorted out of the vehicles by Coronal Alexandra and the twin rotor blades spooled up as we approached.

On board were 4 US NAVY SEALS, some food packs and a few crates of equipment. The noise was still a little loud and he gestured toward some headsets hanging up above 2 empty seats. As I fitted the headset on properly, a voice sounded. "Good afternoon, we are SEAL Team 7. I am Petty Officer First Class Lopez. This is Hall, Carter and Torres", they all nodded in our general direction as their names were called. He continued, "Five minutes until wheels up. If you open the box in front of you as a little token of our appreciation, you will find some treats. Please enjoy them before we fly. Don't be alarmed when you see us escorted by 2 F/A 18E Super Hornets once we are over the English Channel. They're here to protect us not bring us down."

"Thank you", Summer and I said almost in unison as we opened the box. It was a military wooden crate with US NAVY stamped on the side and the presidential seal on the lid. The inside was filled with American Candy. There were Hershey's, Reese's Pieces, American M&M's. It was filled to the brim. There was a note addressed to me. I picked the envelope up, opened it and inside was a handwritten message from the Security General of Defence for the USA thanking me for what I had done for the world. A box full of candy was certainly going to make this journey go a lot quicker. We of course shared with the NAVY Seals and they happily accepted. As I was handing the candy out, the rotor blades spooled to full power and we lifted into the darkening sky towards Geneva for our 3-hour flight.

Just as we took off, my communication device beeped. It was the drone around the swimming pool altering me of the 500-yard perimeter breach. I flipped the app open and saw 6 heavily armed men in unmarked uniforms heading towards the entrance moving slowly and in unison showing a high level of training in the covering tactics they used. They carried AN-94 Assault Rifles It was the Russians again. This time I was going to make sure they were going down. Summer's device had also beeped but she just watched on mine as they went into the building and I lost sight of them. I gave the shoot to kill order and the drone activated the attached gun and passed targeting control over to Al Sal. I received smile and a gun emoji on my cell as confirmation. Summer had now gotten her device out and activated the remote bomb control and was awaiting me to give the word. "Hey, guys", Lopez said, "What's happening over there? We don't normally allow electronics on board." "Sorry", I replied, "but our", I paused for a bit. "Our home is currently being assaulted by 6 Russians but we have a little surprise for them. We will be finished in a second. " ROGER, I want to know all the details", Lopez replied. "OK, you may want to take a look at my phone screen" and the 4 men huddled around. They could see the drone pounding the ground with .50mm Calibre rounds tearing one Russian in half as it hit him. The SEALS looked impressed. I turned to Summer and gestured for the guys to look out the window. I pointed at the rough location of the pool, "Right, go ahead and blow it." The Osprey was now flying just south of the swimming pool and at an altitude of around 10,000 feet. I watched the drone footage as the rest watched out of the window, "This is what revenge tastes like", and with that she pushed a button on her screen. In the distance, we could see a fireball reaching into the dark night sky. There were no survivors.

Lopez tapped me on the shoulder, “Remind me not to piss you off” he said with a laugh. I laughed then had to awkwardly explain what had happened but this also killed some traveling time. I was only interrupted when the awesome sight of 2 Super Hornets joined us about half way over the channel. I even took a picture on my phone and wondered if this would be the last time, I ever would see the UK. Summer was quiet and I could see that she was thinking the same thing. My final task before I was out of range was to self-destruct the two drones and continue eating some chocolate.

Chapter XXI - Geneva

The rest of the flight had been enjoyable. The SEALS loved hearing all of my stories. It felt like a total release after all of these years finally being able to talk people and tell them everything. I had a feeling that after the next few days, I wouldn't be talking to many people apart from Summer. In fact, I don't think my mouth stopped moving for the entire flight. I was interrupted by the pilot, "I've received some bad news from Geneva Air Traffic Control. They have asked us to divert towards Bern and approach from the rough NE across Lake Geneva due to bad weather. So, this flight will be taking a small detour and approx. 20 minutes will be added to our initial ETA."

I heard an audible groan and I wasn't sure if they were bored of my stories or the flight so I decided to stay quiet for the rest of the flight. Once we started to approach the edge of Lake Geneva over the small town of Lausanne, it was starting to get dark. The rain started to bounce off of the side of the Osprey and aircraft moved about as the winds battered it. We had descended to around 5000 feet and I watched as our escort FA/18 Super Hornets peeled off and headed back to base. Through the driving rain, I could see them being replaced by 2 Swiss Air Force Eurocopters and an EC635 helicopter who would escort us into the airport. They closed within 50 feet and yet still all I could make out was the flashing beacons on either side. The visibility was awful. We were now just 2 miles out from the airport and the pilot had issued the warning for us to put on our seatbelts. As he started the final approach over the narrow point of the Lake, I could feel the aircraft start to slow down and the SEALS started packing stuff up around me ready to land. They turned off all internal lights and everything went turned into an eerie red colour for landing. I held Summer's hand and gave it a squeeze mainly out of excitement but somewhat of nerves. I didn't like to fly.

I turned to her and whispered, "I love you" into her ear and as I did, I looked past her and noticed the instrument panel lit up in the cockpit. A loud, audible beeping sound followed the flashing red display of "Missile locked". One of the SEALS jumped up and ran towards the cockpit just as a bright flashed outside of the window followed immediately by an explosion. We were violently rocked to one side. Lopez threw 2 life jackets towards me, "Put these on now". he shouted.

We started to put them on when another explosion jolted us. I turned around to look out of the window just in time to see a huge fireball as one of the Eurocopters exploded. I helped Summer with her jacket as the pilot put the Osprey into a steep bank towards Geneva. The SEAL in the cockpit was thrown to the ground and his head bounced off an internal bulkhead with a loud crack. I could see flares being fired out of the aircraft as it did its bank and we were picking up speed. Just then there was a massive explosion and we were on our side careening downwards fast. "We are hit! Engine lost! We are going down! Brace for impact", I heard over the radio. Smoke was pouring into the hold as the aircraft banked and nosedived towards the ground. Summer was screaming as she held my hand then it all went dark.

I awoke coughing. I felt numb. I shouted for Summer. I looked to the side and could see flaming wreckage all around me. The sound was horrifying. One of the engines was still making noise. I shouted for Summer again but louder this time. Nothing. I tried to get up but I couldn't. My leg was in a lot of pain. This is bad. I felt down my body and there was some metal sticking out of my left leg just below my knee. I could feel a wetness which I presumed was blood. When I lifted my hand back to my face, my suspicions were confirmed. As my eyes adjusted, I could now see that we were in a field beside some trees. Just then, I saw someone coming towards me. I went to grab my side arm. "Shit", I said to myself. It was pure instinct to reach for it but it wasn't there. The figure came closer and I could make out who it was now. It was one of the SEALS carrying what looked like a Colt m4A1 rifle but was limping badly. It was Lopez followed closely behind by Hall who was carrying someone. Lopez knelt beside me, "Matthew, can you walk?" Just then Hall came into view and I could see he was carrying Torres who was very badly hurt. "Is he ok?", I asked out of genuine concern. "Yeah, I'll be fine", Torres said through gritted teeth and in a lot of pain. "Summer is just over there. She's gathering some supplies with one of the pilots", Lopez said. "Thank fuck for that but I think my leg might be broken", I said to him. "No shit Sherlock", he said and he took a closer look. "Yeah, you're not going too far anytime soon. I've radioed for help." He gestured towards Hall, "We need to put up a defensive perimeter now. We have too many injured to exfil. Help shouldn't be long", he barked out orders with a mixture of gestures. This is what these guys were trained for. He grabbed something from his backpack and started bandaging up my leg. His radio lit up after a few seconds but because it was an ear piece, I only heard one side of the conversation. "We have 2 KIA, 1 pilot and SEAL Carter, we have 2 badly injured including Matthew, we have located 4 rifles and a few magazines, we need emergency EVAC now" ..... short pause "OK COPY" he responded.

Just then, Summer and the pilot ran towards us and she hugged me tightly but then noticed my injury. "Jesus, Matthew, and you thought the worst part of today was going to be public speaking", she said with that warm smile I had come to love. "Summer, you

stay with Matthew. Keep pressure on the wound", Lopez said. "You", pointing to the pilot, "Grab a rifle and follow me. We need a defence perimeter while we wait. Torres, you" and he looked at his blood covered, barely breathing SEAL, "Protect these two as best as you can." "Copy that", as Torres coughed and tried to prop himself up. I grabbed my phone out my pocket, and asked Al Sal if there was anything he could do. He informed me that he was working on getting satellite coverage of the area now. We sat there for a few minutes as the rain started to clear a little and visibility improved. It was getting darker but the flames were lighting up the immediate area and I could see Lopez, the Pilot and Hall doing their best to cover all sectors from any further attack. Nothing was being said really as everyone was in shock and had a job to do. Summer was tending to Torres who at this point was unable to speak and was bleeding heavily. She was doing her best to stem the bleeding but she just couldn't with the limited supplies that she had. He drew his last breath as she held him and he closed his eyes and never reopened them. I felt yet more sadness wash over me as Summer held him for a moment, lay him down and came back over to me. "What the fuck happened, Matthew?", she asked. "I have no idea but this isn't a good situation to be in. I must admit I'm scared", and tried to smile. "Me too, Matthew" and she hugged me tightly.
We were interrupted by Al Sal who informed me that vehicles were coming at high speed down the road towards us and flashed the images up on my screen. It quickly became clear that these vehicles were not help as they were coming from the opposite direction of the distant city lights of Geneva.
"Guys this isn't our help", I shouted. Lopez stood up with weapon drawn towards the lead car. The pilot and Hall followed suit. Just then black Range Rovers spread into a 3 abreast formation rather than one behind each other. The three men backed towards me to provide cover for us and started firing towards the vehicles. They

were immediately greeted by a rounds of gunfire which lit up the night sky. Round after round hit the ground behind us as Lopez dragged me behind a rock. Summer, the amazing woman she was, grabbed Torres's rifle and started shooting back. I sat there surrounded by this terrifying sound unable to do a thing. Rounds pounded the rock beside me and gunfire rained both ways but one by one, the closest noises to me fell silent until Lopez and Summer joined me behind the rock. "This is bad, guys. Hall and the pilot are now KIA and it's just us. We are out of options. I count now 6 hostiles moving towards us", his radio lit up. "We are under attack, we need assistance now, 3 more confirmed KIA's", there was a pause, "5 miles out, copy". The sound of helicopter engines drew closer as Lopez kept firing as much as he could but he soon ran out of ammo. Both he and Summer were dry and we were now defenceless and help was a few minutes away. "Matthew", a voice came from behind the rock and had a certain eastern European sound.
"The Russians. How the fuck did they find us so quickly?" Summer said. "Matthew, Matthew, Matthew, come out and play, would you?", the voice said again. His question was followed by what I guessed was a couple of 100 rounds hitting the rock with sharp bits of heated metal landing beside us.

"What's the plan, Lopez?", I turned to him. "Sir, with no weapons, ammo or options, I suggest we try and stall as much as we can while backup arrives." Lopez seemed a lot calmer than I felt. The European voice spoke again, "Matthew, we know backup is 10 minutes out. You have until the count of 3 to come out otherwise, I will kill you all this instant, 1.....2", the voice said. "OK, OK, OK, OK, I'm coming", I said. I turned to Lopez, "Their intel is a little off if they think help is 10 minutes out as it's less than 3 now so I have to stall them as it's better than being dead ", I raised my hands and moved from behind the rock dragging myself since I couldn't walk . "And your two friends. Out you all come now", the voice said. I dragged myself from out from behind the rock and the car headlights were shining in my eyes but I could make out 5 men with guns pointed towards me and one man closer to me with a handgun in one hand and dressed in a long grey jacket, a bald head and a long beard.

Summer and Lopez raised their hands and came out from behind the rock. "Ah, Matthew, we finally meet. I've been tracking you for some time and it's so nice to finally meet you", he said in a smug tone as the lights all went off on the cars and the 5 armed men moved toward us and searched us.
"Clear", one of the men shouted back in another eastern European accent. The assumed ringleader walked towards us. "You", he pointed towards Lopez, "Navy SEAL Lopez, I'm guessing?" Lopez didn't say a word. "You! You just killed some of my men", he lifted his pistol and shot Lopez point blank in the head. "That's what you get!" Lopez's body slumped towards the ground and hit with a thud as the man kicked his now lifeless corpse. Blood started flowing on the ground between us.

"So, Matthew, and you, Summer, we've been instructed to take you with us. Somebody wants you very badly for the shit you've caused them and they are willing to pay handsomely with you dead or alive", he said pacing in front of us. I didn't like the sound of the dead part. "Matthew, on careful consideration and due to the amount of men that have died trying to get you, I'm going to go for the dead option, any final words?" Summer screamed and lunged at him but two men dragged her off and hit her with the butt of their rifles and she fell backwards towards me. He just laughed, "Don't worry, darling, you will be next." The two men then walked towards

me and held my arms back. The man that shot Lopez walked over to me and held the gun to my head. "Any final words? "
I looked at Summer, "I love you, I'm sorry and I hope you can forgive me for getting you into this mess." "Matthew, I have something that I was going to wait and tell you once we arrived in New Zealand to start our new lives together." She leaned over dragging herself off of the ground. Her nose was bloody from the gun's impact and she whispered in my ear, "I love you, too. I'm pregnant Matthew", she said in a soft tone. Those were the last words that I ever heard as I saw a flash of the muzzle and the blackness of death tore through me.

****

I held Matthew's lifeless body in my arms. I was full of rage and my heart was broken. This was no man that just murdered the love of my life in cold blood. He stood there laughing at me at my pain. I stared into his black, soulless eyes. Such hate coursed through me. Four shots rang out around me and his men slumped to the ground. I grabbed a gun closest to me and pointed it towards him. I don't know how many times I pressed the trigger but the anger and rage were strong and I didn't care. The gun clicked to indicate that my ammo ran out. Four soldiers wearing swiss army insignia grabbed me and checked on Matthew and Lopez. One of them helped me up off the ground but I just collapsed over Matthew's body and screamed. My name is Summer and this is my story now.

Printed in Great Britain
by Amazon

49683778R00108